Making the Baby

The Billionaire's Baby Series – Book 2

Ellis O. Day

I love to hear from readers so email me at
authorEllisOday@gmail.com

https://www.EllisODay.com

Follow me

Facebook
https://www.facebook.com/EllisODayRomanceAuthor/

Closed FB Group (sneak peeks, sample chapters, and other bonuses)
https://www.facebook.com/groups/153238782143373

Bookbub
https://www.bookbub.com/authors/Ellis-o-day

Instagram
https://www.instagram.com/authorEllisOday/

Twitter
https://twitter.com/Ellis_o_day

Join My Readers' Group and for a limited time get the entire Six Nights of Sin series for FREE!

www.EllisODay.com

Here's What You Get When You
Join My Readers' Group

Win Before You Can Buy
Exclusive Giveaways
Free Books
Sneak Peeks

Ellis O. Day

CHAPTER 1: ALISON

Anger, hurt and betrayal surged through Alison. Harker had left her on their wedding night to come to La Petite Mort Club.

"It's not what you think," said Harker.

She didn't even bother to respond. She just stood and walked away. She was leaving. She was getting her stuff and going home to her mother's house. She didn't care about the money or Angel Face. She turned down the hallway toward their room. She refused to stay with that asshole for one more second. She stopped at the door to their suite.

"Damn it." She didn't have the key. Her purse, phone, everything was in that room. She looked around for a maid, but the hallway was empty. Forget it. She didn't need her stuff. She'd get the bouncer at the door to call her a cab.

She hurried back down the hallway and into the Club. Harker stood where'd they been, arguing with Ethan. The waitress looked like she was going to cry. The two assholes were probably trying to convince Katie to join them in a threesome. She couldn't believe she'd even considered doing that. The damn man was corrupting her at an epic speed, but the hint of soreness between her legs whispered that it was a wonderfully wicked corruption. She moved along the outskirts of the room, trying to stay out of sight, but Harker's eyes met hers and he headed in her direction. She should stop, be dignified, act like an adult but her legs kept moving and before she could stop herself, she was running. She looked over her shoulder and almost laughed at the look of surprise on his face. He thought he knew her. He thought he knew everything, but he didn't. He didn't know shit about…She slammed into something big and hard.

"Hey, there." Large hands grabbed her shoulders steadying her. "Is everything okay?"

She stared up at one of the biggest men she'd ever seen. "Uh…"

"Are you okay?" The man glanced over her head. "I work here. My name's Damon." He let go of her arms. "You're safe with me. My job is to make sure everyone remembers that the number one rule is consent. Always. No matter what."

"Damon, I'll handle this." Harker's voice was tight with anger as he grabbed her arm.

"Let go of me." She knew that tone. He was furious but too bad because so was she.

"Not until we talk."

"Harker," said Damon. "You heard the lady."

"She's my wife." Harker pulled her to his side.

"Not anymore. I quit." She elbowed him in the ribs.

"Ouch." He tightened his hold. "You can't quit a marriage. You have to get a divorce."

"Fine. Whatever. Just let me go."

"No. We need to talk." He started back into the Club, dragging her behind him.

"Harker, stop." Damon grabbed her other arm, and she had a moment of panic thinking these two large men were going to play tug-o-war with her. "The lady said to let her go."

"And I said she's my wife."

"Who you brought here which means being your wife takes second to consent," said Damon.

Harker looked like his head was going to explode but he let her go. "Alison, come with me."

"No." She stepped closer to Damon, loving the way Harker's eye narrowed. She'd never seen him this angry. Good. Let him feel just a little of the hurt she was feeling. "I'm leaving."

"No, you are no..." He clamped his mouth shut so hard she heard his teeth hit. "Please, let's go back to the room and talk."

"No." She'd never appreciated conciseness before, but every time she said that one little word Harker's face twitched.

"You're overreacting." He glared at her.

"I am not. You...What you did...on our wedding night." Her voice cracked. She hated crying and she wasn't going to cry over him.

"You're accusing me of something that you don't even

3

know happened." He stepped closer.

The scent of his cologne surrounded her, bombarding her with images from last night—him kissing her, holding her, his body hard and hot inside hers.

"I can't believe you're going to leave without giving me a chance to talk to you. To tell you what happened. I expected more from you."

He was right. She didn't know for sure...but..."I want the truth. Did you come here on our wedding night?"

"Come to the room with me and I'll tell you." He held out his hand.

"No." She took a step away from him. "You're lying. You won't tell me the truth."

"Have you ever known me to lie to you? Ever?"

"No...but...Do you promise to tell me the truth no matter what?"

"Yes, if you come back to our room."

She nodded. Damon cleared his throat and Harker glared past her at the giant of a man. Damon's eyes met hers and he glanced at the doorway.

"You are not helping," said Harker.

"I'm helping her," said Damon.

"She's my wife. I'm not going to hurt her."

Damon shrugged. "But you were going to force her to go with you. I want to make sure that the lady can leave if she wants to."

"Oh...thank you." She smiled up at Damon before looking back at Harker and frowning. "When we're done talking, I want your word that you'll let me leave."

4

"I'll even drive you myself."

"Thanks, but I prefer to take a taxi." She was pretty sure Harker's jaw was going to shatter from grinding his teeth.

CHAPTER 2: HARKER

Harker escorted Alison to their room. He'd won the first battle. She was at the proverbial table and ready to listen. Now, he needed to tell her the truth in a way she wanted to hear. He opened the door.

As soon as she stepped inside, she spun around. "Did you come here on our wedding night?"

"Yes." He closed the door behind him but didn't move. He wasn't chasing her through the Club again. If she wanted to leave, she'd have to go through him.

"Yes?" Her mouth dropped open.

He took her hand. "Listen to—"

"Don't touch me." She pulled away from him. "How could you? You lied to me."

"I did not lie."

"You...you said you didn't—"

"I never said that." He may have implied it but that was different. He moved closer. He needed to touch her, to remind her how good it was between them.

"You may as well have. It might not have been an actual lie, but the intent was a lie."

"You wouldn't talk to me." His patience was disappearing fast. "You wouldn't let me explain. You were ready to throw this all away over nothing."

"You came to a sex club on our wedding night. That's not nothing."

"What did you want me to do?" This was not his fault.

"Excuse me? What did I want you to do on our wedding night? I don't know." She threw up her arms. "Maybe stay with your new wife."

"My new wife?" His temper blew and he stalked closer to her. "You mean the woman who had to drink every drop of alcohol she could find to let me touch her but that still wasn't enough, was it?"

"I apologized for that." She backed away from him.

"Oh, that makes such a fucking difference. You laughed at me."

"I...I was nervous, and I apologized and..." She paused, her nose wrinkling in thought. "No. You do not get to make this about me. This is about you." She poked his chest. "You're the one who went to a sex club on our wedding night."

"Because my bride didn't want me, and why do you care anyway? This isn't a real marriage. You sure like to remind me of that, and it's not like you love me." Those words tangled in his throat.

"You don't love me either." She backed away another step. "And I know this isn't a real marriage, but we have a contract. We agreed to be monogamous.

"You..." He stopped himself. This wasn't the time to

correct her about that.

"Were you ever serious about this or was it all some big joke?"

"A joke? If anyone is playing a joke, it's you." He took another step toward her. "I had to bring my wife to a sex club, so she'd see me as a man."

"I...I knew...I know you're a man." She took another step away from him.

"Really? One with a dick or a man like an uncle or eunuch?"

"I...I...You were my boss."

"That's a fantasy for many women but apparently not you." He stalked her across the room.

"No. I never...I..."

"Yes, I know. You never thought of me as a man." That still ripped through his gut like he'd swallowed acid.

"That's not true."

"Isn't it?" He stopped inches from her when her back hit the wall.

"No," she whispered. "I did at first but then..."

"Yeah, that's right. I yelled. You even made a program to laugh about me behind my back."

"How did—"

"You told me all about it. Another gift from my loving wife on our wedding night."

"Oh, no." Her eyes widened. "I didn't...I'm sorry. It's not as bad as it sounds. It's a joke but no one knows but me."

"You're right. It's not bad. Why would I be upset that

the woman I married has her own special program to make fun of me. Hell. She even wrote it."

"I...I'm sorry." Her eyes were huge in her face and filled with apology.

He hated that he was a joke to her, but he hated hurting her even more. He ran his fingers across her cheek and her mouth opened slightly. He wanted to grab her and hold her still while he unleashed his frustrations into this kiss but instead, he kissed her softly. She melted into him and he pressed against her, letting her feel how much he wanted her. How hard he was for her.

"Stop." She pushed on his chest.

He kissed her again, harder this time. They weren't playing but a safeword wasn't only for kinky games. His hands grabbed her breasts, squeezing.

"Harker, stop," she said against his lips. "Debug."

"Fuck," he almost growled before he forced himself to take a step back. It was only a small step, but even that was too much. He planted his hands on the wall by her head, needing to stay close to her.

"I...I can't do this without knowing the truth. I started that contract on our wedding day. From the moment we said I do I was committed to being monogamous with you." She slipped out from under his arm. "I know I wasn't...I didn't make our wedding night easy for you and I...I'll...We can start the contract from here...from last night when we actually...became a couple but only if I know the truth." Her big eyes were so unsure. "I need to know what happened that night."

"Okay. I'll tell you. Nothing at all happened that night." He frowned. "I'm probably the only groom in the history of this planet that didn't get laid on his wedding night." There. Perfect. A little joke and most of the truth. She had to forgive him.

"You didn't"—she waved her hands in front of her thighs—"with someone?"

"No." He took a step toward her, unable to stay away.

"But...but you wanted to?"

"With you." It was true. She'd been his first choice, and nothing had happened so there was no reason to mention Dahlia.

"But you came here so you meant to—"

"Fuck, Alison. What do you want me to say?" He ran his hand through his hair, wanting to tug it out. "I had just gotten married. My wife didn't see me as a man. I was hurt. Angry. Yes, I came here to fuck someone"—he moved closer—"but I didn't."

"Why?" She stared up at him, but she didn't run away, and he was taking that as a win.

"Because I wanted you." That should satisfy her, and it wasn't exactly a lie. He had wanted her on his wedding night; he still wanted her.

"But I was at home."

"Passed out."

"But if you wanted me, you wouldn't have come here."

"Alison, nothing happened." He stared down at her. "Yes, I came here for sex, but I changed my mind." Or it'd been changed for him, but that wasn't important. The only thing that mattered was that he hadn't had sex.

"Why?"

Her and her fucking ten thousand questions. "Because I thought of a way to make you want me."

"What? How?"

"I went to Ethan's office." That was true. "He helped me realize that all I had to do was make you see me as a man, and I could have what I wanted. You." He waited for the softening that his confession should bring but her nose wrinkled in thought.

"So you drove all the way over here and went to Ethan's office to talk to him?"

"No." Fuck. Right now her intelligence wasn't very attractive. "I didn't come here to talk to Ethan. It's just what happened."

"How did that happen? In a club full of beautiful, willing women how did the two of you end up in Ethan's office...Oh." Her eyes widened and then filled with hurt as she puzzled it out in her mind—erroneously again. "It wasn't only you and Ethan, was it?"

He wasn't letting her go down this path. "It was just me and Ethan. I swear." He took a deep breath. "I'll tell you everything."

"Good." She swallowed, seeming even more nervous than he was.

"I already admitted that I came here looking to get laid. I sat at the bar and had a drink. Katie came over and we talked." It was time to sidetrack her a bit. "Her sister is pregnant, and their parents kicked her out. Katie is working extra shifts to pay the bills."

"That's horrible."

He tried not to smile. Alison had the biggest, kindest heart of anyone he'd ever met. "It is." He ran his hands up and down her arms.

"Go on." She shrugged his hands away.

Damn. She was also smart and focused. "Ethan came to talk to me. He was surprised to see me here on my wedding night." He was quite pleased with this rendition of the truth. It wasn't a lie, and it made her feel guilty–a double score for him. "We went to his office and we came up with the plan to bring you here."

"Here? Why?"

"Because apparently, I needed to show my wife some young guy with a huge cock in order for her to want to touch mine." That came out a little harsher than he'd intended but it was true, and it fucking annoyed him.

"I didn't need to see his…penis…but…is that all that happened?"

"Basically. Yeah." There that was the truth too. "We had too many drinks. Did some women bashing but yeah, that was my night. My fucking…Excuse me. Let me rephrase. That was my no-fucking wedding night until I passed out on my couch at home."

"You could've come to bed." Her words were soft and hesitant.

It wasn't in his nature to show mercy. He always went for the win, the kill. "And risk getting laughed at? My pride couldn't take that again."

"I am sorry." She moved a step closer to him. "I…I was just so nervous."

"I don't know why."

She shrugged, stopping right in front of him. "I'm not nervous now." She touched his cheek, and he couldn't help resting his head in her hand. "If you want, we could have our wedding night tonight. You know, a do-over."

He kissed her palm. "I want that. I really want that."

CHAPTER 3: ALISON

"On our wedding night I was in your room, waiting for you." Alison walked into the bedroom. "I think I was at the end of the bed when you entered the room."

"You're forgetting something." Harker's dark eyes roamed over her, making her blood flow thick and heavy through her veins.

"Oh…you're right. I had a drink in my hand." She tried to look serious.

"Let's not relive that part." He moved closer. "I was talking about what you were wearing."

"Oh." She had no idea why she blushed. Yes, that lingerie had been almost see-through, but last night he'd more than seen her. He'd touched and kissed every inch of her body. "I don't have that one with me."

"That one?" His brow raised. "Does that mean you have a different one?"

"Yeah. Ellie made me buy some."

"I knew I liked her." His lips turned up in a sexy grin, making her throb for him. "Get dressed or undressed." He sat on the bed, his dark eyes roving over her body. "I'll enjoy watching you do both."

"You need to leave" She grabbed his hand but tugging on him was like trying to move a truck.

"We don't have to be that literal about recreating our wedding night."

"I know but we're already changing so much."

"Like what?"

"For one thing, I'm not drunk."

"Thank God." He stood.

"And I was going to say that you're not being an ass, but I may have to change that."

"I'm hardly being an ass by not wanting to be laughed out of my wedding bed again."

"That won't happen." She shoved on his back. "Now, go so I can change."

"I'd rather watch." Those words with the hot, hungry look on his face made her body melt like ice cream smothered in warm honey.

"But you're right. If I don't leave, I'm afraid you won't be able to show me your lingerie because nothing is as beautiful as you are naked." He gave her a quick kiss and walked out of the bedroom, shutting the door behind him.

She put her hand over her heart because she was pretty sure it'd just exploded. She was far from beautiful. She was tall with a butt that spent too many hours in an office chair and breasts that were very much on the small side. Her face was at best average in its imperfections—mouth too wide, nose a bit too large and her eyes a plain brown—but when he looked at her all she saw was desire. She was never letting this man go to an eye doctor because he looked at her as if she were the only woman he'd ever wanted.

CHAPTER 4: HARKER

Harker made himself a drink and waited, his eyes going back to the bedroom door time and again. He wanted to watch Alison undress for him, but they could do that later. The idea of redoing their wedding night appealed to him in a basic way.

He'd never considered getting married until it'd been marry Alison or find another woman to have his baby. It was only temporary but the thought of her being his wife, belonging to him made his dick harder than anything had in a long, long time.

What was taking her so long? He glanced at his watch. It'd only been ten minutes, but fuck it, that was long enough. He tossed back his drink, walked to the door, lifted his hand and stopped. He didn't knock on his wedding night. He turned the knob, but it was locked. Shit. Had she changed her mind, decided that she didn't believe his story? The only thing that kept him from panicking was that this was the only door to that room. "Alison?"

"I need more time," she said.

"Oh. Okay." He could deal with that. He made himself

another drink and paced.

She'd be naked by now. She was probably trying to get into some confusing lacy thing with more straps than Psalms in the bible. He certainly hoped she didn't expect him to unfasten all of them. The way he felt right now, tearing them off with his teeth was much more likely to happen.

He'd almost lost her today. It wouldn't have been forever. He could've reasoned with her, convinced her that no anger was worth millions of dollars, but it would've delayed him. He was done waiting for her. He'd waited almost a year. He wanted her and their child. He wanted her body under his, surrounding him, clinging to him. After last night he wanted her again and again and he wanted her now.

He walked back to the door. "Do you need help?" It was the least he could do. She was wearing the lingerie for him. Not that he needed it. Naked was always better—her on the bed with her legs spread and her pussy wet and pink, waiting for him would suit him just fine.

She didn't answer.

He put his hand on the knob and turned. It opened. He stepped inside. Alison stood with her back to him at the foot of the bed like on their wedding night. He put his hand on the door frame to steady himself as all his blood rushed to his dick. She looked exactly like she had on their wedding night—hair hanging loose, that white confection of a nightgown hiding nothing.

She turned toward him. "I found this in my stuff." She

touched the lingerie. "Ellie must've snuck it in my bag. She's kind of a romantic. I know you've seen this one and if you want me to change—"

"Don't." His voice was so thick and rough with need that he barely recognized it.

She was even more beautiful than on their wedding night. She was sober and her eyes were soft with longing. Under the translucent fabric, her nipples pebbled, dark and tight—for him. His gaze dropped to the juncture between her thighs. Was she wet for him too? He was so going to find out.

CHAPTER 5: ALISON

Alison knew exactly what that look of intensity in Harker's eyes meant—pleasure, lots of pleasure. His dark gaze roamed down her body, incinerating everywhere it touched.

"Take off your robe."

"Ah…If we're going to recreate our wedding night, shouldn't you make me and yourself a drink?" That'd been what had happened right before she'd laughed.

"You can have mine." He took two steps and stopped in front of her, wrapping her fingers around the glass. His skin was hot and rough, a delicious contrast to the smooth, cold glass.

She took a sip, wrinkling her nose as the bourbon burned a path down her throat.

"Not to your liking?"

"It's okay. A little strong but okay." She took another sip.

"Let me have a taste."

"Oh sure, we'll share." She handed him the glass and his eyes twinkled with amusement.

"I've tasted that." He bent to kiss her.

"You've tasted my lips too," she whispered, her breath mingling with his.

"It's our wedding night, remember? The only kiss I've had from you ended with a bloody nose."

"I'm so sorry about that." She leaned forward, drawn to his warmth.

"You can make it up to me." He kissed her softly, his tongue teasing her lower lip.

She wrapped her arms around his neck, pushing her body against his but he unhooked her arms and stepped back.

"What? Where are you…"

He walked to the side of the bed and put the glass on the nightstand before kicking off his shoes. He sat on the bed, pulling off his socks.

"Oh. Okay." It was time to get busy. She smiled and started for the other side of the bed.

"Stop." He scooted back and leaned against the headboard. "Take off your robe. I want to see my bride."

They'd done a lot of things last night and today. She already knew he liked to give orders and have them obeyed but she was a bit nervous about this. It was one thing to undress in the heat of the moment and another to strip for him.

"Now, Alison or you'll be punished."

"Punished?" She wasn't sure she wanted that, but her body disagreed. The slow throb between her legs revved up a notch as she remembered the woman on stage last night.

"Yes. Punished." He unbuttoned his shirt partway before pulling it over his head. His dick was already a hard outline in his pants.

Alison's mouth watered. This man's body was enough to wipe all thought from her head. All she wanted to do was touch him with her hands and her lips.

"Come here." He shifted, dropping his long legs over the side of the bed.

"I thought you wanted me to take off—"

"Come here." His voice was rough with passion. "You need to be punished for disobeying."

"Punished how?"

"Use your safeword if you must but until then get your ass over here."

"This isn't at all like our wedding night." She didn't move. She wasn't sure she wanted to do this.

"No, but it's what I wanted to do." He stood and stepped toward her. "You made it more than clear that you didn't want to be my bride."

"I didn't..."

He ignored her. "From the moment you walked into the living room, it was obvious to everyone that you didn't want to be there."

"I'm sorry. I didn't mean..." She backed away, undoing her robe. He kind of had a reason to be upset. "See. I'm obeying. I'm taking off the robe." She let it slide down her shoulders and his eyes darkened from desire.

"Touch your nipples." He stalked closer.

"What?" She backed away.

"Touch your nipples."

Her back hit the wall and he stopped a foot from her. He stared at her breasts and her nipples hardened almost painfully. She ran her hands up her body, squeezing her breasts before her fingers teased her nipples. She sighed as the pull from her fingers throbbed in tandem with the pulse between her legs.

"Move one hand to your pussy."

She didn't even think about not doing it. His voice, his command controlled her body.

"Show me how wet you are." His breath came faster as his hand went to his cock, rubbing it through his pants.

She spread her legs, heat filling her cheeks–part from passion and part from embarrassment. She'd never had a man stare at that part of her body. Her other partners had touched her and tasted her but never just stared. Her fingers slid through her wetness, twirling around her clit.

"I want you naked. Undress."

She stroked herself faster. His dark gaze and gruff voice, pushing her closer to orgasm.

"That's it. You're done disobeying." He grabbed the neckline of her lingerie, ripping the delicate fabric off her body.

She gasped as the cool air hit her heated flesh and her eyes closed as her fingers moved faster around her clit.

"Oh, no. You don't get to come. " He captured her wrist.

"Harker, please." She was so close, just another touch.

"No. Not until you've been punished for your

disobedience."

CHAPTER 6: HARKER

Harker lifted Alison in his arms and headed toward the bed. Later, he might watch her finger herself to release but not now. It was his wedding night, and he was going to be an extremely active participant in all her orgasms.

"Put me down." She wiggled, her hard little nipples burning holes into his flesh.

He couldn't wait to take them into his mouth, biting down on them and making her really squirm.

"I mean it. Put me down."

"Okay." He dropped her legs to the floor and then sat on the bed, his dick straining at his pants.

She frowned at him, seeming surprised that he'd actually put her down. His gaze roamed over her body. She was naked, gorgeous, and all his. He could smell her arousal, hot and musky. He wanted to bury his cock inside her but not yet. First, she needed a lesson in punishment and pleasure.

"You'll have one chance to lessen your punishment, but you have to obey without hesitation and without question."

"That's cheating. You know I'm not good at that." She gave him an exasperated look. "I need to know why, and I want to understand everything before I act."

"I'm quite aware of that." He grinned.

"Then why…You want to punish me?"

"Yes, and after this time, you'll want it too. I promise." He had to make this good for her because he liked to punish. He'd planned on leaving Alison out of that aspect of his life, but that wasn't going to work because she was the only one he wanted to fuck.

"I don't think you're right about that."

"Trust me." He took her hand and kissed her palm. "I mean that." For the things he wanted to teach her, to do with her, to do to her, he needed her absolute trust. "If you trust me, I'll make this good for you. Really, really good."

"And if I don't like it, I'll say debug and you'll stop?"

"Always."

She nodded. "Okay. I guess we can try it."

"Lie down on my lap."

"Lie down?"

"That's not obeying without hesitation."

"This doesn't count. I don't understand what you want. I know how to sit on your lap and straddle your lap but lying down on it?"

"Put your stomach across my legs."

"Oh. Okay, but I don't see the appeal." She crawled across his lap, stretching out on the bed and his legs.

"You will." He already did. The press of her side against his erection made him inhale. All he needed was a little friction and he'd be dripping. He lifted her, shifting her upward until her ass was in the perfect spot for his hand. Her butt was large and soft and so pink that it practically begged for him to slap it. "You're getting your first taste of impact play." His hand landed on her ass, the crack ringing through the quiet room.

"Ouch." She tried to get up. "Why did you do that?"

He pressed down on her back, holding her in place. "You need to obey me." He hit her ass again, hard.

"Hey. That hurt."

"I know." He caressed her butt. She was innocent. He needed to teach her body that this pain was a prelude to intense pleasure.

CHAPTER 7: ALISON

Alison wasn't a fan of this game. It'd hurt when Harker had slapped her ass but from the way his dick pressed into her side, he was really enjoying this. She'd give him a little more time to make this good for her before she stopped him.

"This is the punishment." His fingers skimmed between her butt cheeks. "The pain first and then the pleasure." He stroked her pussy in feather light touches.

Now, that she liked. A lot. Her legs opened, giving him better access but his touches were still light and teasing. She wiggled, trying to give him a hint.

"See how wet you are?"

"That was from before, not from you hitting me," she muttered, her words slightly muffled from the bed.

"Are you sure?" He slipped two fingers inside her.

"Oh…that feels good." She tightened her inner muscles around him.

His other hand landed on her ass. Her body tensed around his fingers and sparks of pleasure pulsed through her. He twisted his hand between her legs and his other hand came down hard on her ass, pushing his fingers against her G-spot. She gasped, almost sitting up as white hot pleasure shot through her body. He did it again and again, his hand landing on her ass and his fingers teasing her G-spot. She pushed up on her arms, wiggling to get away from the pain from his slaps while her pussy clung to his fingers, trying to keep them pressing against her spongy bundle of nerves.

"You're getting wetter." His voice was gruff as his fingers slid in and out. "You like this, don't you?"

He scraped his nails across the sensitized skin of her butt, making her skin tingle as the slight pain morphed into pleasure. She moaned. The sound low and needy as her body surrendered to the pleasure. She dropped back onto the bed, her hips rocking with the rhythm of his fingers. She gasped when he slapped her ass again while his fingers wiggled inside her, teasing her G-spot. She clutched at the bedsheet, jerking forward with his next slap. The movement rubbed her clit against the cloth of his pants and she exploded, screaming as she shattered.

"I know you liked that." He pulled his hand from between her legs, and she whimpered slightly, her body still clutching for something to fill her. He took her arm, helping her off his lap. "Get on your knees."

CHAPTER 8: HARKER

Harker almost came in his pants when Alison obeyed without question. He hadn't planned on letting her come, but it'd been the perfect way to start teaching her body that pain equaled pleasure. She knelt before him, wincing a bit when she sat back on her feet.

"Unzip me."

"Yes, Sir," she said it sarcastically as she rubbed his cock through his pants.

"I prefer Master, but Sir will work."

"Really?" She looked at him like he was nuts. "Master?'

"Yes." He couldn't pull his eyes away from her fingers as she slowly unfastened his pants.

"I don't think I can call you Master." She took his cock in her hand and began to stroke him. Her small, soft fingers squeezing him perfectly. "It makes me think of slavery and that isn't a turn-on for—"

"Sir will work." His hand cupped the back of her head, gently guiding her toward his dick. "Suck it."

"Yes, Sir." The husky quality to her voice went

straight to his balls. She opened her mouth, giving him a glimpse of her perfect pink tongue before her lips closed around the tip of his dick.

The breath hissed through his teeth when she sucked. He grasped the bedspread with both hands, trying to keep from grabbing her head and fucking her face, but damn she could suck dick. She took him deeper, the suction almost making him come as the tip of his cock slid into her throat.

"Fuck." He hadn't expected her to do that, but he wasn't complaining.

She pulled off him, her tongue twirling around his tip. "Did you like that?" Her hot breath caressed his cock.

"Fuck, yes." He had no problem giving praise when it was due, and praise was definitely due for a deep throat. "That was fucking perfect."

"Would you like me to do it again?" Her eyes sparkled mischievously as she licked the underside of his dick, flicking her tongue against that super sensitive spot right below the top.

"Yes." He grabbed her head with both hands. "And I'm going to fuck your face while you do it."

Her eyes widened and a hint of fear mixed with her desire.

"Trust me, Alison. You can pull off whenever you want."

She nodded.

"I want you to touch yourself while you suck me off."

Her hand slid between her legs and her eyes darkened as her fingers began to circle her clit.

"Put my dick in your mouth."

She positioned his cock at her lips, took a deep breath and slid him inside her mouth. His hands tightened in her hair as she lowered onto his shaft, swallowing him.

"Fuck me," he groaned. He held her head still as his hips thrust, her throat squeezing him and making his balls tighten. He pumped into her again. It felt so fucking good—tight and wet. He wanted to fuck her face until he came down her throat. He pulled out a little and then thrust back into her mouth before dropping his hands and giving her control. She stayed like that for another few seconds, her throat tightening as she swallowed and then she pulled her mouth off his cock, inhaling deeply.

"You okay?" He caressed her cheek, staring at the long string of saliva that still connected them like a promise of things to come.

"Yeah." She took his dick into her mouth again.

He dropped his hands to the bed, letting her control it this time. She sucked his tip, teasing it with her tongue. His hips thrust, wanting the pressure, needing that wet tightness. She lowered her head, taking him deep again. Fuck, it felt so good. He couldn't stop himself from grabbing her head and holding her on his cock for one second. She sucked, her throat squeezing him so tight, his balls were going to burst. He wasn't coming in her mouth, not this time. He pulled his dick from her, his chest heaving at the effort.

She panted, her fingers still working her clit as he lifted her and tossed her on the bed.

"Roll onto your stomach." He stood, kicking off his pants. "I'm gonna fuck you so deep and hard you won't know where I start, and you begin."

CHAPTER 9: ALISON

Alison didn't even have a chance to get on her stomach before Harker was behind her. He rolled her over and shoved her legs apart. She moaned as the tip of his hot cock teased along her slit.

"You're so fucking wet." He yanked a pillow from above her and lifted her waist, stuffing it underneath her abdomen. He spread her legs wider and shoved into her in one hard thrust.

She gasped as his cock stretched her. She was still a little sore from last night and earlier today, but her body softened for him, taking him deep.

"Fuck." He grabbed her hair, pulling back her head as he leaned down by her ear. "You were made for me."

His words were as desperate as his body. He pumped into her in long, hard strokes. She rocked her hips, needing to meet him thrust for thrust and feel his hard cock push deep inside her. He let go of her hair and grabbed her hands, sliding them along the mattress until they stretched above her head. His large body surrounded her as he pumped into her over and over, sending sparks of pleasure shooting through her body. The sound of flesh hitting flesh mixed with her moans and his pants, hot and heavy in her ear. He tugged the pillow out from under her, his body pressing down on hers. Pleasure raced through her from everywhere at once—the bed rubbing rough against her clit, his body hot and strong surrounding her, and his cock sliding into her over and over. He held her down, controlling her, dominating her. She was helpless to do anything but receive him, his will and his pleasure. He stilled, his dick filling her, and she clenched on to him. He groaned, seeming to lose control. His strokes became harder and faster, his cock barely leaving her body. His powerful thrusts pushed her forward on the bed, making the mattress rub against her swollen clit. She tried to lift up, but he held her down.

"Let go," he whispered in her ear as he thrust hard into her, pushing her against the mattress.

Pain sparked from her clit and tangled with the pleasure of his cock, and she moaned, her body bucking under his as she came.

He grunted. The sound rough and primal in her ear. His hands clenched hers as he stiffened, exploding inside her. He collapsed on top of her, his hips rocking slowly as he emptied himself into her body.

CHAPTER 10: HARKER

Harker lifted off Alison and dropped to the bed, his heart racing. Sex was always good but each time with Alison was fucking fabulous. He rolled her to her back and pulled her against his side. "I swear your pussy was made for me."

"Gee, you're so romantic."

"I know." He kissed the top of her head. "Don't expect it all the time but this is our wedding night." He leaned over, grabbing the wipes.

"I don't think we would've done that on our wedding night."

"Oh yeah, we definitely would've if you hadn't been falling down drunk."

"Are you going to bring that up forever." She tugged on his chest hair.

"Ouch." He sat up. "I might when it works to my advantage." He tapped her thigh. "Time to spread them, baby."

"Harker, I can—"

"I know you can, but I like to do it." He grinned, quite

proud of himself. "I made the mess. I should clean it up."

"Fine." She opened her legs.

He ran the wipe up her thighs cleaning all the sperm that leaked from her. "You should go and pee."

"I don't have to pee."

"It'll help you not get a UTI." He tossed the wipe in the trash next to the bed and grabbed another one, sliding it over her pussy.

"Okay, I'll try but you know, we could use a condom."

"Makes it harder to get pregnant." He bent and kissed her abdomen and then her pussy. "Plus, I love seeing my cum on you. Inside you. Dripping from you."

"Really?" She stared at him like he was crazy. "That turns you on?"

"It does." His dick was already stiffening a little. He leaned over her, one hand on each side of her head. "No one can say you aren't mine with my cum dripping from your body."

"Possessive, are we?" She ran her fingers across his chest.

"Very." He kissed her and then flopped onto his back. "Now, go pee and get back here."

"Yes, Sir." She hopped out of the bed and he watched her ass jiggle as she walked to the bathroom.

He stretched, pulling the covers up to his waist and waited, an odd feeling of contentment coming over him. He couldn't remember the last time he'd felt like this.

She strolled back into the room and he lifted the covers. She slid onto the bed next to him, wrapping her arm over his chest. His hand skimmed down her back, her skin warm and silky. He caressed her ass and she flinched.

"Ow. My butt still hurts."

He lifted her chin, so her eyes met his. "I'm sorry. Was it too much?" Maybe he'd hit her too hard for her first time.

"No." She shook her head.

"So, you liked it?" He knew she'd come but he also knew that sometimes people changed their minds even if they orgasmed. "All of it?"

"I…I'm not sure." She touched her ass. "It hurt."

He took her hand and kissed it. "It's supposed to but if you didn't like it, we don't have to do it again." He wasn't sure he could go without impact play for too long, but for her he'd try.

"Do you like it?"

"Very much."

"I guess we can try it again some other time."

"Only if you want to." He slid his hand gently over her ass. "You did seem to enjoy some of it, and I think you'll enjoy it more over time." His fingers slipped between her legs. "There's a lot I can teach you if you want to learn." Her pussy was slippery, but he wasn't sure if it was new desire, old desire or even his come. He'd cleaned the outside of her but not inside.

"I'm not ready for the stage or the flogger or—"

"Okay." He rolled to his side, so he could look in her eyes. "I'll take you around the Club and let you watch. We'll see what turns you on and you can tell me what you want to try." He ignored his disappointment at her slight frown. He wanted her in this part of his life, but it was her decision. This was the one area where he wouldn't even attempt to manipulate her. "Or not. It's entirely up to you."

"Oh, no. I want to." She grimaced slightly. "My mom would die if she knew. No, she'd kill me. No, she'd kill you for corrupting me. Then she'd kill me for allowing myself to be corrupted and then she'd die."

He kissed her quickly to stop her from rambling. "Forget about your mom. Do *you* want to experience the Club?"

"I do."

He grinned. He was happier than he'd been in…forever. "This is a much better wedding night than our last one."

"Yes, it is, and I didn't even break your nose." She laughed.

"I was a little nervous about kissing you again. I figured the next time I'd probably be permanently maimed."

"Don't be a baby. It wasn't that bad. Just a little knock on the nose."

He pulled her closer, letting her feel his dick as it stiffened. He stared into her soft brown eyes. He should keep his mouth shut but he wanted to know what went on in that brilliant mind of hers. "If you wanted to see the Club, why did you frown? And don't tell me it was because of your mother. We both know that she doesn't approve of premarital sex but that didn't stop you from doing it."

"I didn't frown."

"You did." He kissed her. "This won't work if you're not completely open and honest with me. I have to know you to know what pleases you."

"Completely honest?"

"Yes." He was starting to get nervous.

"Okay." She frowned again. "I do want to see the Club."

He braced himself for the worst word in the English language—"but".

"We can go whenever you want," she continued. "But I'd rather stay here." She slid her leg over his, opening herself for him. "The Club is interesting, but I like being alone in bed with you better."

Damn, that hadn't been painful at all. "Good because I wasn't talking about tonight." He kissed her because he just couldn't resist. She truly wanted him. "We'll come back next weekend and I'll show you some more, but tonight you aren't getting away from me." His hand drifted between her legs. "I can show you plenty of kink right here."

CHAPTER 11: ALISON

Alison didn't bother to answer as Harker bellowed for her, his voice echoing through the hallway. He knew where she was. They'd left the Club around eleven that morning because even though it was Sunday, he'd had a business call. She'd gone to her office to work and he'd been pestering her since about two that afternoon.

"You'd better be closing that computer," he yelled.

Damn that man. Just the sound of his deep voice was enough to make her body purr, bringing back memories of his lips on her ear saying the naughtiest things before he did every one of them. His large frame shadowed her doorway.

She glanced up from the computer. "You bellowed?"

"Aren't you done yet?" He leaned against the door frame, looking sexy as hell. His five o'clock shadow darkened his lean cheeks. His white business shirt was partially unbuttoned and untucked as if someone had interrupted him while dressing and he wore those blue jeans that made her mouth water. She'd chosen faded ones, but she swore they were already more faded where his cock rubbed against the fabric.

"No, I still have a lot of work to do because someone took me away for a wonderful weekend." She wanted to run across the room and jump his bones but that'd have to wait.

"It's still the weekend. Officially, we're still on our honeymoon."

"True and I'll be done soon."

"You said that at two o'clock and then four o'clock." He looked at his watch. "It's now five after seven."

"Seven? Oh, I'm sorry. I had no idea it was so late. Did you eat?" She touched her stomach. "I'm kind of hungry. You must be starving. I snacked on some pretzels while working. Want some?" She held out the bag to him.

"No, I don't want pretzels. I want you."

"And you can have me." Warmth spread through her body. No one had ever wanted her like this. The man was insatiable.

"Good." He held out his hand. "Come."

"Later. Tonight." She glanced at her computer. "I really have to get this done."

"Alison…" It was clear from his tone that his temper just slipped a notch.

"Okay. I know you get crabby when you're hungry. I'll order something and we'll have dinner." She enjoyed saying "we" like they were a couple. She'd said it before hundreds of times when they'd worked late but this was different. This was a real *we*, at least for a few months.

"I'm not a child."

"Of course not." She rolled her eyes. "Barking at people when you're hungry is what all adults do."

"I'm not barking because…I'm not barking at all. Don't start calling me Barker again."

"I never should've told you that." She laughed.

"You never should've called me that. And"—he strode toward her—"you never should've written a program making fun of what I say."

"I definitely never should've told you about that."

"I said you never should've written it."

"I know." She grinned.

"I may have to get you drunk more often and learn all your secrets." He leaned on the front of her desk.

"I don't think so. I felt like crap the next day."

"Me too." His frown deepened. "But for me, it had nothing to do with drinking."

"Are you going to bring that up forever? It's not a good trait, you know. You should try forgiveness."

"I forgave you."

"Forgive and forget and don't bring it up all the time."

"Someone has a guilty conscience. I wasn't talking about you laughing at me. I was talking about my headache from you busting my nose…twice."

"Oh, come on. That's even worse and I think we're even." She shifted on her seat, pointing to the cushion she'd added to her chair. "My butt still hurts."

"Come and I'll put some oil on it." His eyes gleamed. "I would've done it last night, but I left it at home. I hadn't expected to have to punish you."

"You didn't *have* to punish me."

"But we both enjoyed it." There was a hint of question in his tone.

"Yes, we did." She hadn't exactly liked the spanking part. However, she'd enjoyed being held down and helpless on his lap while he paddled her. The feel of his cock pressing against her hip while his fingers thrust inside her had been kinky and exciting and she'd come hard.

"Good. Then let's go." He straightened and offered her his hand.

"I can't."

"You can." He frowned at her.

"Not yet but I'll order something for dinner and when it arrives, I'll come out and we can eat in the living room."

It was their routine. What they'd done for almost a year. She'd order food and then they'd both sit in his living room and eat while they worked. It was nice.

"No, you work. I'll order the food. What are you hungry for?"

"I'll call. It'll only take a minute." She grabbed her phone off the desk.

"No. I'll do it."

She knew that tone. She could argue all she wanted but he wouldn't budge. That meant she was in for a long night of listening to him complain because he was very particular about his food.

"Don't look at me like I can't order takeout. I survived quite fine ordering food before I met you."

"I'm sure you did okay." She fought not to smile at his

44

dark look. "But you get even crabbier when your food isn't right and then I have to listen to you whine about it all night."

"I don't whine. I just don't like incompetence."

"They can't get it right if you don't tell them what you want."

"Don't blame me for their screwups. I order the food and I expect to get what I order."

"Harker, just let me do it."

"No. I don't want to hear how you would've been done working if I hadn't made you call for takeout."

"I could've been done by now. This is wasting more time."

"Then stop arguing with me."

"Fine." She was going to grind her teeth to dust before the evening was over because he'd mutter and grumble all night when his order was wrong.

"Good. What are you hungry for?"

"I don't care. Whatever." She turned back to her computer. "Call me when it's here."

"Okay. Do you want spaghetti, ravioli or lasagna? Lasagna will take longer."

"Italian?" She looked up at him, wrinkling her nose.

"Apparently not," he said drolly.

"No, that's fine if you want Italian. I'll just have the bread and salad. I'm not in the mood for anything heavy." She'd eaten too much when they'd ordered room service at the Club. The food was extraordinary.

"I'll order sandwiches. Do you want turkey—"

"Sandwiches? For dinner?"

"Tell me what you want me to order." His hands clenched at his sides like he wanted to strangle her.

"I told you. Anything is fine with me."

"If that were true, the Italian food would be here already."

"Oh...please. We haven't been talking about it that long."

"Longer than we should."

"You know what? Surprise me." She turned back to her computer.

"No, tell me what you're hungry for."

"Nope. You pick." She glanced up at him. "You're on your own."

"I'm capable of ordering dinner."

"Yes, but you're not capable of ordering it to your satisfaction."

"I am too." He sounded petulant.

"We'll see." She shouldn't do it, but she so loved to annoy him. He was so handsome when he frowned, all dark and brooding. "But I have a feeling I'm going to break my score on Harker's Barker-Meter." She pressed a button on her computer. "Let's roll the randomizer and see what Barkerism it picks for today."

"Alison." The word was a warning growl.

"Oh..." She laughed. "I already get a point."

"What does it say?"

"Well, it's not exact but it was the intent." She lowered her voice like she was telling him a secret. "Sometimes I'm flexible with the phrasing."

"What does it say?" he repeated.

"Alison, where are you?" she shouted.

"I have not said that today."

"You kind of have." She looked at him, nodding.

"When?"

"Just now. As you walked down the hallway you bellowed Alison!"

"I do not bellow."

"You do too, and since I already got a point for that, I'm rolling it again."

"Don't do it." He took two steps across the room and grabbed her hand.

"Too late." She grinned up at him. "Let's see what you'll say next."

She looked back at the computer, trying unsuccessfully to ignore the bristly man at her side. The heat from his hand and his large presence reminded her of him leaning over her, his fingers tangled with hers as his cock filled her over and over again. Her body almost combusted when the randomizer stopped and she read, "Alison, I need you. Now."

"I want in on this game because you are so going to hear that later," he whispered in her ear.

CHAPTER 12: HARKER

Harker dropped the takeout bags on the coffee table and headed for the kitchen. "Alis…" He shut his mouth. He wasn't going to let her score any more points. "This is such a waste of time," he mumbled as he walked down the hallway toward the business part of his home. "Calling for her is so much faster." He stopped at the door.

She had her head bent, staring at the screen.

"I heard you." She didn't look up. "It still counts."

"How did you hear me? And I didn't even finish your name, so it doesn't count."

"It counts." She glanced at him, her eyes sparkling. She was always in such a good mood. He envied her ability to see the humor in everything. She could take the worst day and make it fun.

"Unless your little program rolled out, *Alis* it doesn't count."

"Okay. I'll concede this time, but I think"—the twinkle in her eyes turned to a gleam—"I'll have to add that."

"Add what?"

"A fraction of my name." She faced the computer, her

hands flying over the keyboard. "Since you've taken an interest in this game, you're going to change your behavior. I can't get my points unless I take that into account and modify my list of phrases."

"You don't have time to rewrite your program. Dinner is here."

"Rewrite? Do you think I just started programming?" She sent him a disgusted look. "The Harker Barker-Meter reads a text file. All I have to do is add"—she began typing—"this line and it's done. It's modified for your new Barkerism."

"That's not funny." He did not bark at her. "And I'll still make sure you lose."

"Wanna bet?"

"I do." Now, he was very interested in this game. He was extremely competitive. His eyes wandered over her, loving how her face flushed. She no longer saw him as a non-sexual male. "What kind of bet did you have in mind?"

"Not the kind you're thinking."

"Shame. That's the only kind worth taking." And the only kind he was interested in winning.

CHAPTER 13: ALISON

"There are other things we can bet on besides what you have in mind." But Alison had to admit, that betting on things to do in bed did have its appeal.

"There are, but none of them are as much fun." Harker held out his hand. "We can talk about our bet while we eat."

The roughness in his voice made her wonder if they'd make it through dinner before they had sex. She had a lot of work to do but she could spare an hour. She needed to exercise more and sex with Harker was a workout, a lovely sweating bout of the most pleasurable calisthenics she'd ever...The computer beeped, snapping her out of her fantasy.

"Ignore it."

"It's done already?" She opened the log file, browsing through the contents. "This is amazing. It ran faster than I anticipated. I need to test—"

"It can wait."

She forced her gaze away from the computer.

"Oh...right. Dinner. Sorry." Her eyes darted back to the

screen. "But this is amazing. I never expected it to work so fast. I still have to—"

"Come with me and eat dinner."

"Right." She knew Harker. He was a bear if she didn't eat with him. She had no idea why he cared because they both spent most of the time working, but it made him happy, or at least less grumpy. "Okay, but give me one minute. I need to get the next batch loaded and—"

"Five minutes. That's it."

"It won't take that long." She turned back to the computer.

"I mean it, Alison. Five minutes."

"All I have to do is change this to point to the source and then change this"—her fingers danced across the keyboard—"and there. Done." She closed her laptop and glanced up, but the doorway was empty. "He could've waited. I told him it'd only be a minute."

She grabbed her laptop and the cord. She'd spend the rest of the evening on the couch working while Harker worked on his laptop in the chair across from her. It wasn't as comfortable as her desk but one time, a few weeks after she'd started working for him, she'd gone back to her office after dinner and Harker had grumbled about it for days.

She walked into the living room. He stood by the couch pulling containers out of a brown paper bag. Her eyes roamed over his wide shoulders and down to his lean hips. Damn, the man was built, and those jeans hugged his ass, making her want to squeeze that tushy and then give it a nip. Later. She needed food and then work and then sex. She put her laptop on the computer table near the couch.

"I got Chinese food." He turned. "Why do you have your computer?"

"I always bring my laptop when we eat." She opened her laptop before grabbing the cord and plugging it into the wall.

"We're having dinner, not working." He sat in his chair.

"We always eat and work." She dropped onto the couch. "Where's your computer?"

"In my office where it belongs. Tonight, we're having dinner and talking like normal people not staring at a computer."

"Uhm…I think most people stare at their phones or the TV or something."

"Then we're going to be better than normal people." He handed her a carton and gave her a quick kiss. "We're going to talk."

"Oh, that's so sweet." She smiled, opening her food. It was Hunan Chicken. He'd gotten her order right. She picked out a piece of baby corn.

"That's me. Sweet." He opened his container, and she leaned forward, dropping her corn into it.

"Thank you." His sexy smirk made her smile widen as she gave him all her baby corn.

"So, what should we talk about?" She ate some rice.

"Whatever you…" He frowned at his food as he leaned back in his chair.

"What's wrong?" She couldn't keep the smugness from her tone. He'd messed up his order.

"Nothing." He dug in the carton. "Except they forgot the meat."

"There's no meat in there?" She knew there was.

"Very little."

"Did you order double meat?"

"No." He glared at her. "Why would I need to order double meat?"

"Because you like extra meat." She took another bite. It was delicious.

"No. I like the amount of meat anyone would expect." He dropped the food back into the container. "Not this sprinkling of meat."

She laughed. "You like meat and a little rice not the other way around. You should've ordered extra meat."

"I would've if I'd known I usually got extra meat." His look and tone were accusing.

"So, this is my fault that you don't know how to order your food?"

"You could've told me you've been ordering extra meat for me."

"I didn't know you were getting Chinese food. Plus, you said you'd done perfectly fine before you met me. If you needed detailed instructions on how to order your food, it would've been easier for me to just do it myself."

"How am I supposed to know how you order things?" He took another bite and frowned, pulling something from his mouth.

"You didn't tell them to hold the water chestnuts, did you?"

This time his look almost incinerated her and not in a good way, but she was used to his glares.

"The first time I ordered Chinese food for you, you made me pick through all your rice with a fork to remove the water chestnuts even though, you never told me that you didn't like them." She'd wanted to strangle him that day, but she'd waited and today she'd had her revenge. She tried to look innocent as she said, "Did you suddenly think you liked water chestnuts?"

"I forgot about the water chestnuts, but I wouldn't have if I hadn't been trying to figure out what food would make you happy. Something that was dinner food, which according to you isn't sandwiches, and nothing too heavy and was…I don't know…How did you put it? Oh, that's right, anything is okay as along as it isn't something I suggest." He shoved more food in his mouth, making a face. He must've gotten another waster chestnut, but he was too stubborn to spit it out.

"I didn't want Italian. What's the big deal?"

"The big deal is that you shouldn't have said you were okay with anything when clearly you weren't."

"I knew you'd be crabby if you ordered." She took another bite of her food. "It's going to be a long night of listening to you." At least she could lose herself in her work. She glanced at the computer. The program was chugging away.

"Close that laptop."

She jumped. "Oh, sorry. I…" Her eyes darted back to the screen.

"Alison." There was a warning in his tone as he took another bite of his food.

"It's just that I have so much to do. The algorithm combining micro expressions with anticipated behavior isn't going that well. I have a lot of work to do if I'm going to make the next projected deadline."

"You're a partner now. Hire someone."

"I'm not a partner yet." She touched her stomach.

"You could be." His gaze followed her hand.

"Oh…yeah." She smiled shyly at him. She could be pregnant right now.

"I'll give you Cormac O'Reilly's contact info tomorrow. Mac should be able to start—"

"You said that I get to hire my team."

"You do. That's why I'm giving you his number."

"I get to pick my team."

"You'll pick him. He's a genius especially with—"

"I'll consider him." She had to fight not to grin at Harker's frown.

"Fine, but I want you to hire someone tomorrow."

"Tomorrow? That doesn't even give me time to interview."

"No need. Mac is perfect for the job."

"Says you."

"I hired you." He continued to eat.

"Merri hired me."

"I approved it. So same thing."

She took a deep calming breath. Arguing with him over the difference between Merri meeting her, interviewing her and hiring her and his approval on a piece of paper wasn't going to help her with this situation. "But this is my team. I'm going to have to work with these people."

"No, these people will work for you.'

"I work for you, but I also work with you."

"You were different."

A small kernel of warmth sparked in her chest.

"I couldn't treat you just like an employee." He closed his container of food. "I needed to get to know you to see if you'd suit as the mother of my child."

CHAPTER 14: ALISON

"Excuse me." Alison dropped her carton of food on the table. That little kernel of warmth turned so cold it could freeze the Sahara Desert.

"What did I say to piss you off?" Harker actually sounded surprised. "You know what this"—he waved his hand between them—"is or was."

"Of course. How silly of me. It's a business arrangement. Don't worry"—she forced herself to smile while inside she crumbled—"I won't forget again." She grabbed her container and turned toward her computer, stuffing food in her mouth so she wouldn't have to talk to him.

"Alison, look at me."

"Nope. Got a lot of work to do." But she did look over at him. "Don't you have work to do?" She put her carton of food on the computer table. This didn't make sense. "You've been pestering me all day to stop working. Why weren't you busy working. You had Friday night and Saturday off too." He should be as behind as she was.

"I had that meeting."

"What did you do after that? You're always telling me how much work you have to do, and you've always got your computer. Every time we eat lunch and dinner, you're working but not today."

"So." He took a drink of his water.

"Why aren't you working?"

"It's our honeymoon. I wanted to spend time with you." He stared at her but there was something hiding in his eyes.

"Okay, fine. You wanted to talk through dinner but—"

"That was a mistake," he muttered.

She ignored him. "Where's your laptop?" He generally worked in the living room at night.

"I told you. It's in my office."

"You said a businessman never stopped working. There was always another investor to find another product to build."

"Yeah. So?"

"So, why are you suddenly not busy." She was still crazy busy.

"I'm not suddenly *not* busy. I still have a lot of work to do but life is about more than work."

"I said that once and you lectured me about putting in the work now so I could enjoy life later."

"It's later."

Her laughter died when she realized he was serious. "You're saying that now is the time to quit working and enjoy life? Why now? Why not a month ago when I said it?"

"Because a month ago if I hadn't pretended to work you would've run out of here like your ass was on fire. The only way I could keep you from leaving was to make you work. Otherwise, you would've been gone. Out with Randy or with Ellie looking for a guy to fuck."

"I can't believe…That's so…You lied to keep me here." Emotions ripped through her. Months of working her butt off—late nights, weekends, holidays—all because he didn't want her to leave. Her brain screeched to a halt. "Wait a minute. You did this so we could be together?"

"Yes." He stood and sat by her on the couch. "I didn't want you finding someone else. I didn't want anyone touching you but me."

"But…" That little kernel was trying to heat up again but what he was saying didn't make sense. "You made me work late almost from the day Merri hired me."

He gave her a dirty look but ignored her jab about who had hired her. "We were behind schedule."

"And you…you started having me stay the night and work late and…Are you telling me you did that all so I wouldn't go out and find someone else?"

"I have no idea how to answer that without pissing you off."

"Then tell me the truth, Harker? Did you purposely alienate me from my friends, my family and from having a life?"

"You make me sound like an abuser, and it wasn't like that." He took her hand. "I wanted you."

"You're saying that you wanted me from the day I

started?" She yanked her hand away from him. It suddenly made sense "Oh my god. You didn't hire me to work on Angel Face. You hired me to have your kid."

"It wasn't like that."

"How did you even know? Did you have someone look into me." She wanted to slap herself on the forehead. "The background check. You knew everything about me before I started."

"We do background checks on everyone."

"But not for their breeding potential." She stood. She had to get out of there.

"Sit down."

She wanted to scream when she almost obeyed.

"Calm down." He grabbed her arm, pulling her back to the couch.

"Calm down?" She jerked free from his grasp. "You manipulated me. Tricked me because you wanted someone to breed little Harkers."

"How did I trick you? I spelled it all out. You signed the contract."

"You tricked me before that. You made me stay here and work so much that I had no life. I practically lived here with no one for company but you. I've been brainwashed. You gave me the contract because I'd finally had enough and was going on a date."

"That wasn't the only reason. I was waiting for the right time."

"You couldn't risk me going on a date, meeting a real guy. You know, a guy who might actually like me." She'd never been so furious and hurt in her life. She'd trusted him—as a lover and as a friend.

"No, I couldn't. Do you know how long sperm can live inside a woman's body?"

"Excuse me?" Her mouth dropped open. He did not just say that.

"Ten days and then I'd have to wait at least two months to make sure that any child you might have in your womb wouldn't belong to this Randy guy."

CHAPTER 15: HARKER

"Don't look at me like that." He wasn't going to feel guilty about this. Alison had known exactly what he'd wanted. Fuck, he'd put it all on paper for her.

"I don't want to look at you at all." She stood.

"Oh, no. You're not running away mad. We're going to talk about this."

"There's nothing to talk about. You tricked me. Manipulated me."

"I didn't do either of those things. I didn't tie you up and force you to stay." Although tying her to his bed had been a frequent fantasy of his.

"You threatened to fire me."

"So? You would've found another job. You're smart, talented, dedicated, personable. You could've worked anywhere but you wanted this job."

Her face tightened and he could see her mind scrambling for an answer.

"So, tell me. How did I manipulate you?"

"Yes, I wanted to work here but not every minute of every day. You made me feel like I had to."

"You did. If you'd put in a forty-hour work week, I would've fired you."

"Why? Was that some kind of test because a mother needs to always be there? Let me tell you a secret. Work isn't a child."

"Stop being emotional."

"Sorry. Being used does that to me."

"I didn't use you. I made you offers, and you accepted them. I offered you a job. You took it. I told you you'd be working long hours and you accepted that."

"You never said anything about staying here all night. Working almost 24/7. Weekends. Holidays."

"You could've declined." He'd done nothing wrong. He'd paid her well, worked her hard and had chosen her to be the mother of his child. She should be thanking him, not berating him.

"I tried."

"Not hard enough."

"The one time I did you—"

"I made you a better offer."

Her jaw was so tight a muscle twitched in her cheek.

"Admit it. I didn't trick you into doing anything. It was all there in black and white. You read the contracts—the one when I hired you to work here and the one before we married."

"You pretended to work."

"Because I wanted to get to know you better." He softened his voice, appealing to her feminine side. "I wanted to spend time with you."

"Only because you wanted someone to have your child."

"Not only." So much for thinking she'd be like any other woman. "I knew you were smart, but I wanted to know what kind of person you were. I wanted my child to have a shot at better genes than I could give him…or her. I wanted the woman I chose to be kind and funny and love life. I don't want my child to be exactly like me."

"You didn't have to lie and say you were working."

"Didn't I? I asked you once if you wanted to grab dinner and—"

"You did?"

"Yes, I did." Another perfect hit. He'd asked her out and she didn't even remember. "A few weeks after you started working here. I went out of my way and got reservations to that Mexican fusion restaurant you'd been talking about for weeks."

"Oh. Right. I had plans. You could've tried again."

"I did. I asked you out on New Year's Eve and you asked me to get more tickets so you could bring friends."

"That was supposed to be a date?" Her complete shock was another direct hit to his ego.

"What did you think? It was New Year's Eve. The only other holiday more known for dates is Valentine's Day but I wasn't trying that one. You would've probably had me invite every single person you knew."

"Don't try and make this my fault. You were already making me work all the time. I even worked Christmas Eve."

"We had a deadline and I liked having you around, although right now, I have no idea why."

"You liked knowing my uterus wouldn't be housing any sperm."

"That too." He shifted closer. "I helped your friend move. What guy would do that unless he was trying to impress a woman?"

"You said you wanted to make sure I got back to work as soon as possible."

"Because you treated me like a friend. You didn't even see me as a man on our wedding night."

"That has nothing to do with this."

"It has everything to do—"

"No. You didn't have to trick me and lie to me about working."

"Fuck, Alison. How else was I supposed to keep you with me? Asking you out hadn't worked. This was the only thing that did."

"That's not an excuse."

"No, it isn't; it's the truth."

"Well, unlike you I actually have work to do." She grabbed her laptop and walked back to her office.

CHAPTER 16: ALISON

Alison stared at her computer. For the first time in her life she was unable to lose herself in her work. The conversation with Harker tore through her head, whipping her emotions into a storm. She felt used, manipulated and stupid because Harker hadn't actually lied. He'd pretended to work but he was right. If he'd given her the option, she would've left or worked in her office.

She hated that her heart did a little flip when she thought about all he'd done to get to know her better. He said it was because of his child, their child, but was that really all? She was an open person. It shouldn't have taken him long to know she was kind and giving. Yet, he'd spent almost a year doing whatever he could to keep her by his side.

She closed her computer and left the business part of the house. She stepped into the living room. Harker was sitting in his chair, his laptop open in front of him. He glanced up at her, his eyes wary.

She walked behind him to the couch so she could see his computer. "You're playing video games?"

"Yeah."

She sat on the couch. "Is this what you did all those nights I was working until my eyes crossed?"

"Sometimes." He shrugged. "Other times I did work and some nights I just looked shit up. I take it you're not mad anymore."

"I'm not happy."

"I'm not happy either but that's not the same as not being pissed."

"You're lucky I'm a very logical person. If I were like Ellie—"

"We wouldn't be here because I don't want a woman like her."

"Hey." No one said anything bad about her best friend in front of her, but that didn't stop her from wanting to jump up and do a victory dance. Ellie was gorgeous and every guy Alison had ever dated would've dropped her in a second for Ellie.

"You want me to want Ellie?"

"No, but you can't say anything bad about her either."

"I didn't. I said she isn't the kind of woman for me."

"And I am?" Her heart quit beating, waiting for his answer.

"I chose you, didn't I?"

That wasn't exactly what she'd wanted to hear.

"Come." He stood and held out his hand.

"Oh, no." She knew that look. As much as she wanted to take his hand and let him lead her to paradise, it wasn't time. "You're not getting off that easily.'

"Are you making a jab at my performance?" His eyes sparkled. "There were only a few times that it was fast, and I always made sure you came first."

"Not that." She laughed. By his cocky smirk he knew damn well she wasn't complaining about his performance.

"You said couples should forgive and forget," he said.

"I did and I will when we're done."

"I thought we were done."

"Hardly." She sat up straighter. "You may not have tricked and manipulated me by a dictionary definition, but you came very close."

"But I didn't cross that line."

"That's debatable but forget all that."

"Gladly." He held out his hand. "Let's go to bed and make up."

"You did lie to me."

"Jesus." His arm dropped to his side and he tipped back his head as if seeking divine intervention. "I did not lie."

"You said you were working when you weren't. That's a lie."

"I don't recall ever actually telling you that I was working."

"Harker." She wasn't in the mood for his verbal games.

"Okay. I may have said it. I don't remember but I'm sorry. Is that what you want to hear?"

"Yes, and that you won't do it again."

"Fine. Are we good?"

"Is there anything else that you've lied to me about? If there is, now is the time to tell me." She braced herself, hoping she could handle whatever he confessed.

"You actually believe that the time to tell you other shit that'll make you mad is when you're already pissed at me?" He shook his head. "I'll never understand women. The only good time to admit a lie is when you're caught."

"So you have lied to me."

"No. Not that I remember."

"You lie so much you don't remember?" She had no idea how she was going to live with a man like that.

"No, but maybe one day I said I liked your perfume and didn't."

"You don't like my perfume?"

"That's not the point." His jaw clenched and that muscle in his cheek started dancing.

"I think it is. I don't want you gagging when I come near you."

"I love how you smell." He sat next to her. "Especially your pussy when you're aroused. It's musky and—"

"Go sit in your chair." She pushed his shoulder because if he stayed there talking like that she was going to climb onto his lap and ride him like a racehorse.

"I like it over here better." He leaned against the back of the couch. "It's much more comfortable." He stretched out his arm and pulled her against his side.

"Stop it." She tried not to laugh but a playful Harker was her weakness. "I mean it. Go back to your seat so we can finish this discussion."

"Good God. The conversation that never ends." He got up and dropped back down on his chair.

"Which perfume?"

He stared at her as if she'd grown another head.

"I want to know. Which perfume didn't you like?" She needed to throw it out. She didn't want him ever not liking how she smelled.

"I don't know. It was something you got from your mom for Christmas."

"Vanilla Cream? You don't like that?" She loved that scent. It made her think of baking and the holidays.

"Not really. Makes you smell like one of the foster homes that I lived in. The lady baked all the time but us fosters couldn't have any of the treats. They were for her real kids."

"Oh. I'm sorry." Her heart tore in two at what he'd gone through. She'd done research on him before she'd accepted the job offer. There'd been one or two lines in an article about how he'd grown up in foster care. There'd been nothing about his experiences and he never spoke about it. "I won't wear it again."

"It's not a big deal. It doesn't make me gag or anything."

"It is a big deal. It makes you sad and I won't wear it again. I have other perfume." She hesitated. "I wish you'd said something to me."

"I just did."

"That doesn't count. You only told me because I made you. I guess, I can understand why you didn't say anything.

We weren't dating, but we were friends. You should've told me. I wore that for months." She felt horrible. He must've been so sad every time she'd been near him. "You need to tell me from now on. I know you don't like talking about that part of your life but—"

"I don't and I think we should talk about our bet."

"Our bet?"

"Yes. On your little program."

"The Harker's Barker-Meter? You were serious about that?"

"Very."

"Okay. What kind of bet?" She was pretty sure he'd want something sexual and she was okay with that, better than okay. She had to stop herself from squeezing her legs together to sooth the throbbing in her pussy.

"What do you want?" His voice had grown huskier. It was the same sound that whispered in her ear as he thrust inside her.

She wiggled on the couch and his eyes sparkled. She was so out of her league when it came to sex games and him. "Ah…you go first."

CHAPTER.17: HARKER

Harker's dick hardened. Finally, they were getting to the good part of the night. "If I win you agree to do anything I ask you to do. Even if you don't think you'll like it, you'll agree to try it."

"You mean sexually?" Alison's voice cracked a little.

"Yes." He pushed down his annoyance, reminding himself that trust took time. He'd been in a relationship with her for almost a year, but she'd only joined two days ago.

"You want me to do something that I don't want to do? I thought it was all about consent with"—she waved her hand at him—"you people."

"Us people?" He should be offended but instead he burst out laughing. "And who are us people?"

"You know…kinksters or whatever you call it."

"I call it people who enjoy sex."

"Most people enjoy sex, but they don't have to tie people up or hit them."

"I bet most want to try. They're just scared…of your people." He smirked.

"My people?" She pointed at herself.

"Yes. Those who pass judgement on things that they don't like or don't understand."

"I don't do that."

"You just did when you labeled me and my people as a group of kinksters. Whatever that even means."

"I didn't mean anything bad, but you've told me over and over that pleasure is all about consent. Now, you want me to do something you know I don't want to do."

"No, I'm asking you to keep an open mind and try new things. If at any time you don't like it—and you have to be honest with me about this—then you use your safeword and we stop."

"Oh…uhm…"

"I won't ask you to do anything that I don't think you'll enjoy. My pleasure is in giving you pleasure. I want to teach you things that'll make you come so hard you'll shatter in my arms." His cock throbbed in anticipation of her surrender. He had so much to show her.

"Uhm. First, how will this game work?" Her voice was soft, hesitant but he could see her pulse beat fast in her throat. "How will we pick who wins?"

"We run a contest Monday through Friday. We'll use your program—"

"Harker's Barker-Meter," she corrected.

"Fine but let me say that I hate that name."

She shrugged. "Seems to be a thing with you. You hate Gus too."

Oh, she was so going to pay for that. "As I was saying,

we'll roll…Harker's Barker-Meter and if I say that phrase anytime during working hours that day, you get a point. Otherwise, I do."

"That's not fair. You just won't say it."

"According to you, I can't control myself." This victory was his.

"That won't work. You can't know the phrase until after you say it. That's the only way it's fair."

"No. You could change it."

"You don't trust me?" She feigned being insulted.

"For this? No. I know how competitive you are. You'll have to write it down in a text file. It'll have a date/time stamp."

"That'll work but it'll have to be on my computer."

"On the network."

"Where you can look at it? No. No way." She shook her head.

"You don't trust me?" He threw her words back at her.

"Not at all." She grinned.

He leaned forward. "We'll have to work on that because I need you to trust me for us to enjoy the things I want to do to you."

"I…I trust you with that stuff. I know you'll stop if I say debug…but no gags. I have to be able to say debug."

"Gags have their own rules, but that's fine. No gags." He liked hearing her moan and gasp when he fucked her.

"Okay."

"Good. It's all settled. You'll pick a phrase every morning. If I haven't said it by end of business, then I win, and we have a great evening."

"Every day? That won't work."

"Why not?"

"Something new…in bed…every day? That's a lot of new. Once a week. Winner of three out of five."

"But we will have sex every day, right?" Actually, this way would give him time to earn her trust.

"Yeah, but nothing super kinky. Nothing like you're thinking."

"You have no idea what I'm thinking."

"I've been to the Club. I have some idea."

He laughed. "You haven't seen anything. I'll show you around the next time we go."

"When is that?"

Fuck. He loved how excited she was. His sweet, innocent Alison was a kinkster at heart. "Saturday. After I win this bet. Now, come here."

"Wait. I haven't told you what I want."

"You can tell me over here." He was done talking.

"I don't think we'll do much talking if I go over there."

"You always talk."

She laughed. "Okay. Correction. You won't do much listening."

"I'll do enough. Now, come here or do you want another punishment?" He'd happily give her another spanking. Maybe he'd even tie her up this time.

CHAPTER 18: ALISON

Alison stood, unable to deny Harker or herself any longer. She walked toward him. "You know, you're lucky I'm so forgiving."

"I am. Take off your clothes." His eyes traveled down her body, stopping at the juncture between her legs. "Start with your pants."

"Getting right to it tonight, I see." She undid her button. She was as eager as he was, the intensity on his face making her wet and achy.

"I've been waiting all day." His eyes darkened as she slowly pushed her pants down. "Underwear too."

"Do you like them?" She ran her hands over the pink lace, letting her fingers slide a little between her legs. "Ellie made me buy them."

"I like them very much." His eyes almost gleamed as he stared at her fingers. "But I like your pussy better. Now, take them off."

She pushed her panties down and kicked them away.

"Undo my pants," he said.

She stepped forward, bending and gliding her hands up

his thighs. His breath grew heavier as she teased him, moving slowly up his body to his belt. She unfastened it, making sure she brushed her fingers against his cock every chance she got. Finally, his pants were undone, and his dick strained against the fabric.

"Take it out and lick it."

"Yes, Sir." She started to kneel.

"Did I tell you to kneel?"

"No, but I thought—"

"Don't think. Just obey."

"I'll try, but that's not exactly in my wheelhouse."

His chuckle died as she pulled his dick from his pants and wrapped her hand around his shaft. His dick was long and smooth and so hot. She ran her tongue up his length, flicking the sensitive underside softly before taking the tip in her mouth.

"Look at me while you suck my cock." He gently pushed her hair from her face.

Her eyes locked with his and her pussy throbbed at the need and pleasure in his gaze. His mouth opened slightly, and his chest heaved as she sucked and worked his shaft with her hands. She pulled off him. Licking around the top before taking him back inside and sucking hard, letting the tip press against her throat.

"Fuck, Alison." He grabbed her arms. "Come here."

CHAPTER 19: HARKER

Harker lifted Alison onto his lap. She spread her legs, rubbing against the length of his cock. He was done with games. He'd been horny for her since they'd left the Club that morning. He positioned his tip at her entrance, sliding it through her wet heat. Her hands rested on his shoulders and their eyes locked. A faint blush of arousal covered her cheeks and her warm breath mingled with his.

He grabbed her waist with one hand and pulled her down as he thrust upward, sheathing himself inside her. She gasped, squeezing his shoulders, her body instinctively trying to pull away from his invasion.

"Shhh. That's it." He held still, letting her get used to him. "Tell me when you're ready."

"I'm a little sore from last night…and this morning." Her lips tipped upward. "I was a bit overused by my husband."

"Overused? Hardly. I went easy on you."

"Easy. I lost count of how many times we—"

"It would've been more." He thrust a little, moving gently inside her. "I could fuck you all day and night."

"Yeah?" She rocked back and forth on his dick, her eyes drifting partway closed as she rubbed his cock against her G-spot.

"Yes." He grabbed the back of her neck, pulling her to him for a kiss. "You're perfect. Made just for me."

"Yeah?" This time it was softer, hesitant.

"Yes." He meant it. He'd fucked a lot of women and none of them had felt like this. "Now, ride my dick. I need to see what you like." He gently slapped her ass and her pussy clamped around him. "And you pretend to not like impact play."

"I think you're corrupting me." She smiled.

"I'm training you."

"I thought you said I was perfect?" Her pace increased as she rolled her hips finding the spot that made her eyes drift half-shut and repeating the motion.

"Your pussy's perfect. You need lessons."

"Hey." She stopped moving.

"You'd better find your release because I can only take so much before I lose control"—he tangled his hand in her hair—"and then it'll be hard and fast." He thrust as she rolled forward, so his cock hit that spot harder than when she worked his dick by herself.

"Oh...Do that again."

"Your wish is my command." He guided her hips, setting a slow rhythm like she'd done. He pumped into her, watching her closely until he found the motion that made her gasp softly.

She moved faster on his cock, her body squeezing his

more and more as her rhythm increased. His fingers tightened on her hips as he thrust into her every time her hips rolled forward.

"Oh…oh…yes, Harker. Right there." She ground against him her fingers digging into his arms as her body tensed, clamping around his dick like a wet, velvet vise.

His eyes dropped to her tits. Damn it. She still had her shirt on. He grabbed her T-shirt, shoving it and her bra out of his way. Her small breasts jiggled, a sheen of sweat on her pale skin. She rode him hard and fast, her movements becoming desperate. She was close and his balls tightened as her body clasped on to him, tighter and tighter. He lowered his lips to her breast, sucking that luscious flesh into his mouth before biting down on her nipple.

Alison screamed and bucked, arching away and pushing her pussy down hard on his cock. He wrapped his arms around her, holding her body to his as he fucked her in hard, fast jabs, searching for his own release. Her pussy squeezed him rhythmically, making his nuts tighten. His fingers dug into her hips, holding her still as he came, spilling himself inside her.

CHAPTER 20: ALISON

Alison ran her hands through Harker's hair, his face still pressed against her chest as his hips slowly thrust, emptying ever last bit of his sperm inside of her. Shit, it made her horny just thinking about it. Having a man come inside her was still such a new experience.

Before Harker she'd always—ALWAYS—used a condom. None of her relationships had been long-term enough for her to go without. The dual protection of birth control and condoms was a lot better than an accidental baby and a mother who'd die of embarrassment, or at least moan about it for the rest of her life.

He kissed the side of her breast before lifting his head. "You good?"

She smiled at him. He wasn't gentle during sex but afterwards he was so sweet. She kissed him. "Yeah. It was great."

"Even this?" He tweaked her nipple.

"Ouch." She wiggled, his dick still buried inside her. "That hurt."

"Sorry." He licked around her nipple, the warmth of

his mouth soothing the sting.

"I don't believe you." The sight of his dark head at her breast and his hot mouth teasing it, made her body tighten again. She continued stroking his hair. It was so thick and soft, a complete contrast to the rest of him—all hard muscles.

He kissed her nipple and his dark eyes met hers. "I never want to hurt you, except for pleasure. Did you like it?"

"I think you know that answer." She'd come so hard she'd almost bucked off his dick.

"I need you to tell me. Just because your body reacts like I expect it to, doesn't mean that you enjoyed it."

"Really? I would've thought that was exactly what it meant."

"Not your brain." He cupped her cheek. "Your body I know how to please. Your brain, I'm not sure." He seemed so sincere and so confused.

"You're doing a good job so far." She kissed him softly, but he captured her head and held her still while his tongue invaded her mouth and made desire flood her body again. She melted against him, unable to withstand the force of his passion. She was his to command and to mold. Her arms wrapped around his neck as he stood. "What are you doing?"

"Taking my bride to my bed." He shifted, letting his pants fall and then kicking them aside. "You know we haven't fucked there yet."

"Again? Already?"

"I'll need some time, as you can tell." He pulled her hips closer, his dick semi flaccid but still inside her. "But that'll give me more time to get to know you."

"I think you know me pretty well after this weekend."

"Not even close. I need to find every erogenous zone you have and that means I need to explore every inch of your body."

"Oh…" She shivered as his finger slid between her ass cheeks. "Every inch?"

"Yep. Every inch." His dark eyes gleamed.

CHAPTER 21: HARKER

Harker skimmed his hand up and down Alison's back as she lay tucked against his side. He'd just spent the last two hours making her come over and over until he couldn't take any more and had found his own release.

He could die a happy man except then he'd never get to fuck her again and that wasn't going to happen. He was addicted to her. He hadn't felt like this since his first foray into dominance and submission. He'd been the sub and had been absolutely devoted to his domme.

"You're going to cheat." Alison's fingers played in the hair on his chest.

"What the hell?" He looked down at the top of her head. The way her mind worked fascinated him but not when it pulled shit like this. "Where the fuck did that come from? I haven't even looked at another woman since we went to the Club."

"Oh, no. Not like that." She laughed, looking up at him. "I didn't mean you'd cheat with another woman."

His ire eased a bit. "Then what did you mean because I'm not into men?"

"No. No. Not sexually. The bet. I don't trust you not to cheat."

"The bet?" He had no idea what she was talking about.

"Yeah. Harker's Barker-Meter."

"I hate that name." He hated that she'd made a game out of his desire to have her near him.

"Sorry, but that's its name. It's better than the Harker-Meter, right?"

"Not when your nickname for me is Barker."

"It wouldn't be if you'd stop barking orders at me."

"Maybe I would, if you'd do what I told you to do."

"Hey, I get my work done." She sat up. "Speaking of that, I wonder if the program finished. Since I changed that algorithm it's been running super-fast. I need to—"

"You need to stay right here." He grabbed her arm and tugged her back to his side.

"I really do have a lot of work to do." But she snuggled closer to him.

"It can wait."

"Not with a boss who barks at me." She lowered her voice in her awful imitation of him. "Alison, is module four done? Have you started the bug fixes on module two yet?"

"You're hiring someone tomorrow." He was done with this. She needed to spend time with him and working while he watched her covertly wasn't going to work for him anymore.

"No, I'm not."

"This is why I bark," he grumbled. "You never obey."

She leaned on his chest. "I'm sorry but I can't hire

anyone tomorrow."

"Fine this week."

"No."

"When then? I already have a few candidates for you to choose from. Mac is perfect. Hire him and then pick another couple of people."

"I'll look at the resumes…Wait a minute. Why do you have candidates already? You hadn't mentioned that you were planning on expanding."

He did not want to answer that question.

"Harker, tell me the truth." Her eyes narrowed.

"I wasn't sure what would happen after I asked you to have my child. I had to be prepared to replace you."

"You were going to fire me if I refused?"

"No." Then he shrugged. "Probably not. You might have quit."

"Probably not? Oh, I should've refused and then sued you for sexual harassment."

"Too late for that now." He slapped her butt playfully. "You're my wife. I can sexually harass you as much as I want."

"No. That's still not allowed but"—she kissed his chest—"you can sexually harass me as much as I want."

"As long as you want it a lot."

"I do." She rested her chin on her hands. "I think I've decided what I want if…when I win our bet."

"Talking to you is like traveling through a maze." It was definitely brain calisthenics because she zipped from topic to topic.

"You should be used to it. You know my mind jumps around."

"I do but that doesn't make it any less confusing."

"Well, it should and stop trying to change the subject."

"I'm not. Why would I bother? You'll be on another one soon enough."

"I will not." She gently tugged on his chest hair. "Back to the bet. First, I think we need to change the game because otherwise you'll cheat."

"I'm offended you think that but how do you think I'd cheat?"

"You'll just not speak to me for three days."

"That's not cheating as long as I don't look at the phrase of the day." Damn, she was too freaking smart. That'd been his plan.

"The Barkerism of the day," she corrected. "And it would be cheating."

"I disagree." It'd be winning and he was all for that.

"That's why we're changing the rules."

"Are we?"

"If you want me to play, yes we are."

"I definitely want to play with you." He'd already planned their night at La Petite Mort Club. All he had to do was talk to Ethan tomorrow and make sure the man was agreeable.

"Then we change the rules."

"To what?"

"I'll install the program on your computer. You'll make up a list of things that you think I'll say. We each get ten on our list and we remove one once it's picked."

"Do we get to add new ones?"

Her nose wrinkled as she thought it through. "Yeah, I think that's fine. Each list will always be ten phrases."

"Deal." He could still win this. "I'll put my Alison-Ramble—"

"Hey, it's not nice to make fun of me." Her eyes twinkled with amusement.

He ignored her. "On the same file share. We can each see the date and time stamp, so we know no one cheated and we'll password protect the file so the other one can't get in it."

"Perfect. If you say the phrase that I pick before I say your phrase, I win. And vice versa."

"What if neither of us says it?" he asked.

"Hmm. We'll extend the time from when we start work until we fall asleep. If neither of us say it by then it's a draw and no one gets a point."

"I think we add to the list then."

"What do you mean?"

"For example, if tomorrow I pick that you'll say, *I can't wait to suck Harker's dick* and then—"

"Please pick that one because I won't be saying that…ever."

"As I was saying, if neither of us say the phrase then we run the program again after adding a new phrase like, *Harker has the biggest dick I've ever sucked.*"

"Again, please pick that one." She laughed. "I know I'm not going to be saying that at work or at home. I'm going to win every week."

"You might say it, because I know it's true." He grinned. "But the point is there will be two points up for grabs the next day."

"Deal." She smiled at him. "I'm really looking forward to playing."

"I'm looking forward to winning."

"In your dreams."

"We'll see." He rolled over, pinning her beneath him. "I never lose, Alison. Never."

"You've never played against me."

"I've played with you and we both won. We'll both win again when I claim my reward every week."

"You are so cocky."

"Getting there." He rocked his hips, letting her feel his dick along her thigh.

"Aren't you even curious about what I'm going to want when I win?" she asked.

"It doesn't matter because you won't win." He quickly kissed her to stifle her protest.

CHAPTER 22: ALISON

The next morning Alison hurried into Harker's office. She'd spent way too long choosing the ten phrases that she knew Harker would say for their bet.

"Hey. Sorry I'm late." She sat on one of the chairs at the table where Harker, Merri and Tobias were seated. Her face heated slightly when her gaze landed on Harker. This was the first time she'd seen him in a professional manner since they'd had sex and all she could think of was him naked, his body moving above hers, inside hers.

"No problem," said Merri. "We were just going over the promotional materials for one of our other products."

"Let's get star…" Harker stopped, his eyes darting to Alison.

She plastered an innocent expression on her face. That wasn't one of her phrases, but she wasn't going to let him know that.

He'd made her install the program on his laptop last night while they were in bed. She'd tried to get him to fill out his ten phrases, hoping she could get a peek, but he'd refused. He'd already been in his office when she'd gotten up this morning. He'd texted her that his Alison-Ramble for the day was picked and on the shared drive.

He cleared his throat. "I believe it'd be a fabulous idea if we proceeded with the agenda."

Alison choked back a laugh. Harker was blunt and to the point, not flowery and overly polite.

"I've asked Merri to run the meeting this morning," said Harker.

"What?" She should've expected this.

"You heard me."

"So, you're not going to be…talking?" Her phrases had been based on this meeting. Harker always barked that they needed to work harder, meet this deadline and several other things like that.

"Of course, I'll be talking…if needed."

"You can't do that."

"What's going on?" asked Tobias.

"Nothing," said Harker.

"It's not nothing," she said. "You're cheating. I knew you'd cheat."

Harker's grin made her stomach drop to her toes. He spun his laptop toward her. He had his text file open. "One point for me. Only two more to go." He turned to Merri. "On second thought, I will run the meeting today."

CHAPTER 23: HARKER

The next afternoon, Harker sat in his office studying the new proposal Tobias had given to him. Business was going well. Actually, everything was going exceptionally well except Alison had been avoiding him. She'd claimed she was busy working but he was pretty sure she just didn't want to lose another point. The good thing was that she couldn't win a point without seeing him.

Someone tapped on his door.

"Yes.' He looked up from his computer.

Alison slipped into the room, glanced behind her and then quickly closed the door.

"Is everything okay?" This wasn't like her. She usually entered a room like a whirlwind, throwing the door open and blowing across his office but today she was hesitant.

"Yes. Of course." She smiled but her lips quivered.

Many of his employees had been in the office today meeting with Merri for training on the new timecard application. If someone had said something to hurt her, he'd fire them. "What's the matter? What happened? Did someone say something to you?" He stood and started across the room.

"Nothing now." This time her smile was real. "A point for me."

"What?" He stopped.

"Check my file. My password for today is *Harker is a loser*. All one word and all lowercase." She turned to leave.

He lunged across the room, his hand slamming on the door, closing it as his other hand spun her around. "Using my concern for you to win a bet is very underhanded."

She stared up at him, a wide grin on her face. "You started this." She patted his cheek. "I didn't want to play this way but like you, I'll do whatever it takes to win."

"I'll remember that." He grabbed her hand, kissing her palm and letting his tongue dart out to taste her. His cock rose as the sparkle in her eyes turned into heat. "And I'm going to remember this too." He bent, capturing her mouth with his as his hand slid up her waist to her breast.

"Harker," she muttered against his lips. "We can't. Someone will hear us."

He trailed kisses along her cheek to her neck. "You should've thought of that before you came in here and tricked me." She arched into his touch as he teased her nipple through her shirt, pinching the hard, little bud.

"I didn't expect this. I didn't come in here naked or anything."

"You should've. It would've saved me some time." He lifted her shirt. "Raise your arms."

"Harker, we can't." But she lifted her arms.

He pulled the shirt off her head, tossing it onto the

floor.

"Janice is still here. I just saw her talking to Merri."

"Is that what's taking Merri so long." He pulled her breasts out of the top of her bra, propping them up like the most delicious treats ever.

"What are you talking about?"

"Merri and I were having a meeting. She'll be back in a few minutes."

"Wha…ohh" Her protest turned to a moan as he sucked her nipple and teased it with his teeth.

"You'd better be quiet," he said between kisses. He undid the button on her jeans. "They're going to hear you." He slid his hand inside her pants, rubbing her pussy before slipping one finger inside of her panties. "You're so wet. Are you wet for me all day?"

"Yes." Her hips thrust against his hand.

"Fuck." He was going to explode. His mouth captured hers, his tongue invading and demanding her surrender. She was his and he needed her now. "Kick off your shoes." He lifted her, shoving her against the door as she tried to push off a shoe. Her thighs squeezed his hand as he stroked her faster.

"Oh god, Harker." She panted, her hot breath teasing his ear.

He bent and yanked off her shoes before pulling down her pants and underwear and tossing them aside. He straightened, grabbing her thighs and wrapping her legs around his waist.

"Hold on." He reached between them and unzipped

himself, freeing his cock.

He kissed her, letting his tongue slide into her mouth as his dick slid into her pussy. She felt so good—wet and tight. Her pussy clinging to his cock as her legs squeezed his waist. He thrust into her hard and fast and she gasped against his lips.

"Look at me." He grabbed her face as he moved inside her.

Her eyes fluttered open. They were hazy with passion. He grabbed her breast, teasing her nipple with his thumb and finger. Her mouth opened but she bit her lips to stifle her scream. He wasn't letting that happen. He didn't give two shits who heard them. He fucked her harder, their bodies thudding against the door and her soft whimpers fueling his lust. She clung to him, her nails digging into his back. Her eyes locked with his and he fell into their softness. He never wanted to leave. He grabbed her face and kissed her, claiming her mouth as he claimed her body. She moaned as he pinched her nipple, her thighs trembling around his waist as she came. Her body tightened around him, squeezing his cock. Jolts of pleasure streaked through his body. He buried his face in her neck, his fingers digging into her thighs, holding her still as he thrust into her over and over until he exploded.

"You are mine," he growled in her ear. He held her pressed against the door for several minutes as her hand trailed up and down his back and shoulders. He'd stay like this all day if he could, but it wasn't possible. "I have to say, that's the first time I almost don't mind losing," he mumbled against her neck.

"Almost?" She laughed softly. "I'll have to try harder next time."

"You will." He swatted her ass. "Start by wearing a skirt. I need easier access."

"I don't think you do. This isn't going to happen again at work."

"Wanna bet on that?" He grinned. "I'll win that bet too." His chest swelled with pride at her soft sigh when he pulled his cock from her body. "I can't wait to see you walk out of here." He tucked his dick back into his pants and zipped up, her legs still wrapped around his waist.

"You want me to leave?" she stared at him in confusion.

"No." He kissed her quickly. "But if they didn't hear us, they'll know what we did by the way you walk."

"They will not." She sounded horrified.

He stepped back, letting her slide down to the floor, smirking when her legs wobbled.

"I'll walk just fine." She leaned against the door as she straightened her bra. "Give me a tissue." She held out her hand.

"Spread your legs." Harker couldn't pull his gaze from her pussy, glistening with her arousal as his sperm trickled down her thighs.

"Harker."

"I can't tell if you're disgusted or turned on and I don't care." He stepped back and leaned against his desk. "Now, do what I said and spread your legs."

"I can't believe you want to see this…It's messy…and…" She widened her stance.

He grabbed some tissue and strode toward her, stopping so close that her breasts touched his chest. His gaze locked with hers and then he knelt. Her pussy glistened, pink and perfect, right in front of his face as his cum dripped from her body. He ran the tissue up her thighs wiping away his sperm. The muscles in her legs quivered at his touch.

"There's some here." He stroked her pussy with the tissue from front to back and almost smiled as her hands clenched into fists at her sides. "I bet there's some here too." He dropped the tissue and spread her labia, inhaling the fragrant scent of sex. He leaned forward, letting his breath tease her sensitive flesh before licking her, twirling his tongue around her clit.

"Oh…god…Harker." Her hands dug into his hair.

He sucked her clit, and she shivered. He grabbed her hips holding her still as he feasted, licking and sucking before sliding his tongue deep inside her, tasting her need and his sperm. He kissed her thigh, nipping it gently. Her hands tightened in his hair, trying to guide him back to her pussy, but he gave her one last kiss, long and slow before he stood, his mouth only inches from hers. "There. All clean."

"Oh…but…" She blinked at him, confused.

"I told you I hate to lose." He kissed her quickly and turned and walked toward his desk.

"You…you…did that on purpose. You ass."

Something hit his back. "Ow." He turned around and her shoe was on the floor next to him. "You threw that at me." He hadn't expected that.

"Yes, and I feel a little better." She pulled on her pants and grabbed her shirt from the floor. "And just so you know, I'm not going to be in the mood tonight." Her jaw jutted out stubbornly.

"Good. I enjoy making you change your mind. Just so you know, we will fuck tonight, and you'll beg me to let you come."

"Ha. Not tonight, buster." She yanked open the door. "Oh, ah...Hi, Merri."

Merri stood right outside, half-turned as if walking away. She turned. "Oh. Are you two done?" Her eyes sparkled with laughter. "I was going to come back later but..."

"Nope. We're done." Alison glanced at him. "We are so done."

"For now, but not tonight." He laughed at the finger she waved at him over her shoulder. "Yep, that's exactly what you'll be doing."

Her hand dropped so fast he could've sworn it had a brick tied to it.

CHAPTER 24: ALISON

The next day, Alison had everything planned, but she needed Tobias' help. She found him in the office kitchen. "Hey, I need you to do me a favor."

"What kind of favor?" He bit into his sandwich and looked at her like she was holding a bomb.

"Oh, come on. I can't believe you don't trust me.

"I trust that this has something to do with Harker."

"Yeah, it does, but it's nothing bad. We're playing a game and I want to win."

"Is that what all this *a-point-for-me* has been about?" He took another bite of his sandwich.

"Yeah."

"What kind of game are you two playing?" He held up his hand. "Forget I asked. I do not want to know. Please, I'm begging you to fight your desire to ramble on with an explanation."

"Okay." She laughed. Those kinds of comments used to hurt her feelings, but that stopped when she accepted that she did talk a lot. "I won't explain but I need your help to win."

"Win what?"

"The game."

"I don't know, Alison. This is your thing not mine." He finished his sandwich.

"Please. I need to win because I want to know more about Harker."

"You've spent every day with him for almost a year. You know Harker."

"I don't know anything about him before I met him."

"He's taken you to the Club. You know him better than most." He picked up his trash and tossed it into the garbage.

"I mean when he was growing up. I know his father was never in the picture and his mother died from an overdose, but that's basically it. He grew up in foster care and put himself through college."

"Then you know everything there is to tell."

"That's bull."

"Look. If you want details about Harker's childhood, you'll have to ask him." He grabbed a bottle of water from the fridge.

"That's exactly what I plan to do." She grinned. "With your help."

"Sorry. I'll pass." He started to walk away.

"Wait." She grabbed his arm. "You lived with him in college. You know how he is about losing."

"He hates to lose. He's the worst loser I've ever met. He's a grown man and still freaking acts like a toddler when he loses."

She almost had him. "And if I win, Harker loses."

"He'll be furious and then he'll pout like a giant baby."

"Yep, and you'll get to enjoy every minute of it."

"I'm in." Tobias grinned. "What do you want me to do?"

CHAPTER 25: ALISON

About thirty minutes later, Alison lurked in the hallway outside Harker's office. It was one of their rules that the other person had to hear the phrase. The fact that they said it couldn't be delivered second hand.

Tobias was already in the room giving Harker an update.

"When do you meet with the new clients?" asked Harker.

"Tomorrow," said Tobias. "I'll let you know how it went."

Alison held her breath. The trap would be set soon. She leaned against the wall by the door.

"Oh, Harker." Tobias' voice was closer. He must've walked to the door. "I have extra tickets to the opera on Saturday. Do you and Alison want to go?"

"No. You know I hate the opera. I have no idea how you and Merri can stand listening to people screeching in a foreign language."

"Because we enjoy culture and adult things. Have you ever considered that Alison might like to go?"

Alison cringed. What was Tobias doing? She'd coached him for twenty minutes, but he always wanted to add his spin.

"Alison? She doesn't like opera," said Harker.

"Are you sure?"

"Yeah. I'm sure." Harker sounded bored. He was probably already looking at the computer.

"Did you ask her if she liked opera?"

Tobias was messing up everything. This wasn't going to work. She'd have to figure out another way to get Harker to say her Barkerism of the day.

"I don't need to ask her. I've spent enough time with her. I know what she likes."

Alison rolled her eyes. That man was so sure of himself. She couldn't wait to win this bet and see the surprise on his handsome face when he lost.

"Come on. The woman might like something you don't know about or maybe she wants to try something new."

"She doesn't."

"You don't know that." Tobias sounded disgusted.

"I know that if I ask her and she wants to go to the opera I'll be stuck going. So, I'm not bringing it up."

Damn it. Alison wanted to scream. She should've gotten Merri to do this, but she was closer to Merri and Harker might've been suspicious.

"Harker take some advice from a man who's been married a long time. Ask her. I'm begging you. Save yourself a fight and ask Alison if she wants to go."

"No."

"You'll be sorry if you don't. The two of you need to talk about things besides work."

"Like opera? I'll pass."

"No. It doesn't have to be opera. Talk about things you like. Your feelings."

"Are you running a fever? Do you even know me? I don't have feelings and I certainly wouldn't talk about them if I did."

"Yes!" she shouted and then clapped her hand over her mouth but that didn't stop her giggles.

"Son of a bitch," said Harker.

She popped into the doorway. "Score another point for me." She almost jumped with excitement. "One more and you're going to answer all my questions. Anything I ask and I have a lot of questions."

"You..." Harker's eyes darted between the two of them. "Tobias, you're a traitor and you"—his gaze locked with hers—"this means war."

CHAPTER 26: ALISON

The next day Alison sat in her office debugging some code. She stretched. Where was Harker. It was getting late, and he hadn't come by to pester her about going home.

It was his daily routine and her chosen Barkerism for today was based on this. All she needed was one more point and she'd win for the week. She couldn't wait to learn about his childhood. She knew it hadn't been good, but it had turned him into the man he was today. She wanted to know everything about him-the good and the bad. She glanced at the time. It was almost eight o'clock. Where the heck was he?

The soft rumble of his voice drifted toward her office. She turned back to the computer, pretending to work. Victory would soon be hers. She changed a bit of code. No sense in wasting time. This part of the program was giving her a lot of trouble. She couldn't get the algorithms to work right. They kept misreading the guilty or shady looks on faces for confusion or nervousness.

"And this is Alison Harker. My wife." Harker's deep voice filled the office. "You'll report directly to her."

She turned as Harker walked into the room followed by a young, geeky looking guy. He was thin, wore an old sweatshirt and worn jeans. He had black hair and thick glasses that almost concealed his intelligent green eyes.

"Alison, this is Cormac O'Reilly," said Harker.

"Hello." She smiled and stood, holding out her hand to the young man. She was going to kill Harker. She'd told him she'd contact any possible new hires.

"Hi. It's great to meet you." The kid shook her hand. "And call me Mac. I can't wait to start. Harker's told me so much about the project and the speed that you're getting is amazing." His eyes darted to her computer. "May I have a look?"

"Ah…no." She closed her laptop. "This is proprietary."

"He's already signed the non-disclosure papers," said Harker. "Mac has access to everything."

"What?" This time she didn't try to hide her annoyance. Mac would just have to deal with it.

"He'll be working mostly nights. He has classes during the day. Mac's going for his second doctorate. It was easier to give him full access. Plus, I trust him." Harker nodded at the kid. "I've known him for a few years now."

"Since high school," said Mac. "Harker helped me get the scholarships so I could go to college."

"That's great." She forced a smile. "But can you excuse us please?"

"Sure." The kid glanced between the two of them.

"We'll only be a minute." She hated making the guy

feel unwelcome. She knew that feeling too well. Programmers were notoriously competitive, and no one wanted anyone smarter than them at the office. Since she was usually smarter than everyone else, she'd often been made to feel unwelcome.

"Go ahead and log in." Harker pointed to a spare laptop that sat on a table in the corner. "Tobias gave you your account information, right?"

"Yeah." Mac walked over and grabbed the laptop.

"The network drives should be mapped. You can find the code under Angel Face—"

"Harker, we need to talk." She was going to strangle the man. She gave him a look that meant they had to talk now as she strode out of the office.

"Get familiar with what's been done and—"

"Now, Harker." She grabbed his arm as Mac sat and opened the laptop.

"We'll see you tomorrow." Harker didn't budge as she tugged on his arm. "You'll be here around four in the afternoon, right?"

"Yep," muttered Mac, already focused on the computer.

"Tomorrow?" She pulled harder on Harker's arm. "No, we'll see you in a few minutes." She hated firing the kid because of Harker's blunder but she would.

"Okay," Mac mumbled, his fingers flying over the keyboard.

"Don't change anything." She wanted to yank that laptop from him. It was her code. Her baby.

Harker gave her a funny look. "Change whatever you need to but make backups first and note what you changed so you and Alison can discuss it tomorrow."

"Harker, I mean it. We need to talk." She stormed down the hallway. She was going to kill him…slowly.

CHAPTER 27: HARKER

As soon as Harker closed the door to his office. Alison started in on him.

"What do you think you're doing? You actually hired him? To do what? Because he's not working on Angel Face. What were you thinking?" She almost shook with anger.

He kept his face impassive as he walked to his desk. "I don't understand your question. Or more precisely, I don't know which of the hundred questions you asked me, you want me to answer."

"Which…You don't understand…Let's start with why Cormac O'Reilly is in my office and why he thinks he works here?"

"Great. Two questions I can answer at the same time. Because I hired him today." He sat behind his desk.

"You hired him?" Her face flushed, and her eyes snapped with anger. "That was my job." She poked her chest, drawing his attention to her breasts. "Mine."

It'd take work to ease her out of this pique, but he did love a challenge. "And I told you to hire him." He stood and walked over to her, taking her hands. "You need help. I'm tired of you working late every night and then collapsing into bed."

"After sex. Don't you dare try and say that I'm not upholding my part of the contract."

"That's not what I meant." He cupped her face. Fuck, he was falling hard for her and it both terrified him and made him so freaking happy. "I want to spend time with you besides when we're fucking but you're always working."

"Don't." She slapped his hand away. "Don't try to make this into something it isn't…something sweet. You told me I could pick my team."

"I also told you to hire someone, and you haven't. You keep putting it off."

"I'm waiting."

"On what? You can't do this all on your own."

"I know that." She almost bristled.

"Then why are you so pissed? Mac is perfect. He's young, enthusiastic, and an expert in programming artificial intelligence. The one part of Angel Face where you're struggling. He can help."

"I understand all that, but the point is, it was my job to hire my team, not yours. You had no right to do this. None."

Harker winced slightly. He was pretty sure he was going to be sorry about this, but he really did like to win. "Ding. Ding. Ding. A point for me."

CHAPTER 28: ALISON

"You did this to win the bet?" Alison almost screamed.

"Not *just* to win the bet." Harker reached for her, but she backed away.

She didn't want him touching her…ever. "I can't believe you…you did this. You broke the contract."

"I did not break the contract." His eyes hardened. "I'd never break the contract."

"Never. Ha." She threw up her hands. "You were going to break it on our wedding night when you went looking for sex."

"I didn't break the contract then and I didn't break it now. It states that you can hire your team, but it doesn't say that I can't hire someone for your team. What's not in the contract is as important as what is. I'm surprised your lawyer didn't mention that."

"Oh…well, he didn't." She hadn't bothered to hire one.

"You didn't hire one, did you?"

"It doesn't matter. I understood the contract. I paid a lot of attention to the monogamy clause and even you have to admit that you almost broke that one."

"Not even close."

"You went to a sex club to have sex." She rolled her eyes.

"That doesn't violate the contract."

"I suppose you're right. Going and planning to have sex doesn't but if you had…"

"Enough." He held up his hand. "Please tell me why you believe I almost broke the contract today."

"I don't think it. You did break it because it's my job to hire my team. By you hiring Mac, you're the boss, not me." Again, she hit her chest when she really wanted to hit him.

"You're still the boss. I even told Mac he'd be reporting to you. The contract doesn't state anything about whom I can or cannot hire." He turned toward his desk. "Do you want me to get it for you so you can re-read it because you obviously didn't understand it the first time."

"I understood it. I hire my team. Since I didn't hire Mac, you need to fire him." She turned and strode to her office. She stopped in the doorway, but Harker wasn't behind her.

Mac looked up from his computer, his green eyes almost shining behind his glasses. "This is fabulous. I never would've thought to do this." He pointed at the screen as he ran his other hand through his wavy black hair. "I have so much to learn. I was thrilled when Harker told me that I'd be working with you."

"Oh…thanks…uhm." Now, she felt like a shit. None

of this was Mac's fault.

"Are you going to work more tonight? I have a ton of questions and Harker mentioned that you were having some issues with the AI. We can look at that if you'd rather. Whatever you want."

"Ah...no. I just came by to say goodnight. You can email me your questions so we can talk about them when you get here tomorrow."

"Okay. Sure." He turned back to the computer, lost in the world of code.

She wanted to slip into that world too. It was difficult and frustrating at times but never as confusing as real life. She went back to Harker's office. "Don't fire him. He shouldn't suffer because..."

The room was empty. She walked into their house and found Harker in the kitchen, reheating leftovers.

He glanced at her. "Do you want pizza? Thai or Mexican?"

"You weren't going to fire him, were you?" It was clear he'd had no intention of doing what she'd said.

"No." He put some of three different types of food on two plates. "He's perfect for the job and you'll realize that once you get over your fit."

"My fit? This is not a fit. You overstepped."

"I own this business. Hiring the best person for the job isn't overstepping." He carried the plates to the table.

"You said I could do it. It's my team."

"Then why didn't you? It's been almost two weeks since we married, and you haven't even started looking to hire anyone."

"Because I'm not their boss yet."

"Is that what this is about?"

"Don't make it sound like it's silly because it's not."

"No, but it is easy to fix." He put utensils on the table for both of them. "I'll send out a memo making you the manager of the engineering team."

"You can't do that."

"Why not?"

"Because that could destroy my reputation."

CHAPTER 29: HARKER

"Destroy your reputation? I'm promoting you. That helps your reputation." Harker opened the refrigerator and grabbed two bottles of water.

"You're not listening," Alison said through clenched teeth.

"I am listening to you, but you're not making any sense. Officially promoting you to manager of the engineering department is the best solution to this situation and it can only help your reputation." He sat at the table. Problem solved.

"What if I don't conceive? There's no guarantee that I will and if I don't this whole deal goes away."

"That won't happen." He wanted a child with her, not with anyone else.

"You don't know that. I wasn't tested for fertility. You weren't tested for fertility."

"There's no reason to think about this, let alone talk about it." He stuffed some food in his mouth.

"There is now because by hiring Mac or worse, making me the official boss and then taking it all away when I don't conceive will destroy my reputation. I'll be the woman who was promoted for being your wife. You have no idea how hard it is for a woman in business, especially IT. With every promotion there are whispers about how she used sex to get the job."

"You're worrying about nothing. Everyone here knows you deserve this position. Plus, you'll conceive."

"Stop saying that like you know. You don't. I don't. My mom only had one child. My aunt had none. Neither of us know for sure if I'll conceive."

"The odds will be better if you quit getting mad at me."

She snorted a half-laugh. "Then stop doing things that piss me off."

"I thought I had." He leaned forward, putting his elbows on the table. "I hired Mac so you don't have to work so much. I want us to spend time together."

"We do spend time together." Her eyes softened.

"Working. I want us to do other things."

"Like what? Ever since I've known you, all you do is work." Her eyes narrowed. "Or pretend to work."

"Exactly. I don't want to pretend with you anymore." Not about anything, including their marriage.

"Me either." Her words were quiet and the warmth in her eyes filled his heart. "But please talk to me next time before you do anything stupid."

So much for the warmth. "It wasn't stupid but I'll talk to you next time." He scooted his chair to the side and took her hand in his. "Now, come over here and let's seal this agreement with a fuck."

"The term is seal with a kiss." Her expression was part amused and part exasperation.

"We'll do that too." He kissed her hand.

"No." She pulled from his grasp. "You're not getting off this easily."

"I could be if you'd come here and sit on my lap." He patted his legs. "We haven't had sex in the kitchen yet."

"And we aren't going to tonight either."

"So you want to go to the bedroom?" It was worth a shot.

"No. We're not having sex."

"You mean now. Right?" He leaned back on his chair. She might be saying she was still mad, but she wasn't. All he had to do was charm her and his cock would be buried inside her in no time.

"At all tonight."

"Do you want to conceive or not?" He ran his hand over his dick. "I'm pretty sure I've got the lucky load right here."

"Good god, you're unbelievable. Where do you come up with this? Is there a class men take? Sure Fire Ways Not To Score or What To Say If You Don't Want To Have Sex."

"We don't need a course." He laughed. "We just need to say what we're really thinking. If you women knew what actually went through our heads, we'd never get laid."

"And you've decided to let me see inside that sick skull of yours."

"Peek. I've decided to let you peek." He patted his thigh again in case she'd changed her mind.

"I'm so lucky." Her eyes dropped to his legs and she shook her head.

"You are. It means I trust that you're as horny as I am, and you'll find what I'm thinking hot and not disgusting."

"You're wrong on both points. You may want to try being a gentleman instead."

"Nope. Raw, hot truth works best with you." He leaned forward again. "For example, right now, I'm trying to figure out if that mark on your shirt is your nipple or a play of the shadows. If it's your nipple then you're getting turned on and soon you'll be shifting your legs because you're starting to realize how empty you are without my cock inside you."

"Oh my god." She turned and walked toward the door.

"Wait. Aren't you hungry?" If he kept her in the room, he'd eventually convince her to fuck him.

"No. I'm tired." She turned, giving him a look that if they were cartoons would incinerate him on the spot. "I'm going to bed. Alone."

CHAPTER 30: HARKER

A little later, Harker crawled into bed. Alison was on her side as far away from him as possible. He almost laughed. He'd cross a freaking ocean on a raft to get close to her, the width of his bed was not an obstacle. He scooted over and tossed his arm around her waist.

"Harker, I told you. We're not having sex tonight."

"I must not be doing something right if you think this is sex." He pulled her against his body.

"This is a prelude to sex and we both know it." She squirmed to get away, making his dick harden at the feel of her soft ass pushing against him. "See. If this isn't you trying to have sex than what's that?"

"That's your fault." He rolled his hips, pushing his dick against her softness. "I'm always like this around you." He kissed her ear. "Only for you." It was true. He didn't want anyone but her.

"Well, that's too bad for you tonight." She elbowed him in the gut. "Get off me."

"Ouch." He tightened his hold on her. "I'm not on you. If I were, you'd know because my dick would be buried inside you."

"You're on me enough." She elbowed him again. "Move."

"Damn, that hurts." He let go of her and rolled to his back. Her elbow was pointy.

"Good. I told you. No sex."

"Come on. I can't believe you're still mad at me."

"Still mad at you?" She sat up. "It's been what? An hour since you—"

"Since I what?" He sat up. "Tried to help you? Because that's all I did." He touched her cheek. "I don't like you working so much."

"Yeah, I was thinking about that." She pushed his hand away. "It sure is convenient that this bothered you so much that you had to do something about it when you could also win a point."

"I saw an opportunity to take care of two situations at the same time." It was the smart thing to do, but he was pretty sure she didn't see it that way.

"You saw an opportunity to win another point. That's the only reason you hired Mac now."

"That's not true."

"I don't believe you."

"You should because it's the truth." Fuck, she was annoying sometimes.

"I will if you forfeit the point."

"So that's it." He shook his head. "I can't believe you'd pretend to be upset just to win this game."

"I'm not pretending."

"You weren't this upset earlier in the kitchen."

"Because I fell for your line about wanting to spend time with me."

"That's not a line." Now, he was pissed. "If anyone should be pissed, it's me. Hiring Mac will be a huge help to you, but do you appreciate it? No. Instead you're angry and withholding sex." He almost brought up that refusing to fuck him did break their contract, but that was one of the safety measures that he'd only use if the deal blew up.

"You're unbelievable." She flopped back onto the bed.

He stared at her. She was really mad, and sick fuck that he was, it was turning him on. "You know, angry sex is hot." He stretched out on the bed, very close to her. She might be curious enough to give it a shot.

"You're disgusting."

"Try it before you judge." He tossed the covers back so she could see how aroused he was. "Tempers hot. Sex rough and selfish. You take what you need, not worrying about if I like it."

"Thanks, but I'll pass."

"Okay, but you really should try it at least once in your life."

"I will. With my next husband."

He ground his teeth together. The thought of her with another man made him almost explode but raging at her wouldn't get him what he wanted. "It won't be as good. It'll never be as good as you and me." His gaze locked with hers and there was a flare of desire in her eyes before she stamped it out.

"It'll be better because we'll love each other, and we won't hurt each other to win a bet." She rolled away from him.

"Don't pretend like you've been playing fair. You were the first one to bring another person into our game."

"Having Tobias help me was nothing like what you did, and you know it." Her voice cracked.

"I don't know shit. All I did was hire someone you were told to hire days ago. He'll take a lot of the workload from you. You should be thanking me."

"I am so done with this conversation." She sat up, grabbed her pillow and tossed the covers aside.

"Where the hell do you think you're going?"

"To my room." She started to climb out of bed.

"No." He grabbed her am. "We're married. We sleep together, pissed off or not."

"Let go." She tried to pry his fingers from her forearm.

"Lie down and I will."

"No. Let go of me," she said through gritted teeth.

"Alison, please just lie down. I won't touch you, but I mean it. We're married—"

"It's not a real marriage."

"It's real enough." He was tired of hearing her say that every time they disagreed. "We should sleep together always, mad or not."

"We're not having sex so why do you care where I sleep?"

"I don't know." It annoyed him but he did care. They were married and that meant she slept with him.

"That's not a good enough answer."

"Fuck you." He let go of her. "Then go. Leave. I don't give a shit." He rolled onto his side. He couldn't force her to stay. No one stayed unless they wanted to and no one ever wanted to stay with him.

She got out of bed and walked to the door.

"I care because I like having you by me." He had no idea why he'd said it except that it was the truth.

"What did you say?" She turned toward him.

"Nothing," he muttered. He hadn't meant to say it the first time. He definitely wasn't repeating it.

She walked back to the bed. "No sex and no touching."

"Got it." He rolled onto his back and stared at the ceiling as she settled on the bed next to him. The huge lump in his throat stopped him from speaking but in his head, he whispered, "Thank you."

"Good night, Harker."

"Night, Alison." He closed his eyes. It wasn't perfect. He wanted to touch her, hold her, fuck her, but he'd survive as long as she was next to him.

CHAPTER 31: HARKER

Harker woke slowly, the scent of Alison filling his head and his dreams. His dick pressed against her warm ass and his hand clutched the satiny skin of her breast, her nipple a hard bud against his palm.

He buried his face in her neck, and she moaned softly. He moved his hand downward, sliding under her shorts and between her thighs. Fuck, he was horny, and she was already damp. He stroked her pussy, coaxing the wetness from her body as he kissed her neck, feeling her pulse beat under his lips. She sighed, her hips gently rocking into his touch. He pushed her shorts down to her knees and guided his cock between her thighs, rubbing his tip through her wetness. She moaned, reaching up and running her fingers through his hair.

"Open for me." His voice was gruff with need as he pushed his cock inside her and her body clung to his.

"Oh…" She stiffened, her hand stilling on his head.

"Fuck, you feel so good." Her legs were still together, making the access for his dick even tighter. He thrust into her and then pulled almost all the way out before surging forward again, her body tightening around his.

"Harker…oh…" She gasped as he pressed on her abdomen, making his next thrust push against her G-spot.

He slid into her in long, hard thrusts, her body clasping onto his.

"Harker, stop." Her hand pulled at his hair.

He kissed her neck, his hips moving faster and faster as his balls tightened. He was close. "It's okay, baby. I'll wait for you." But he wouldn't last long. His fingers found her clit and he rubbed that hard little bud, making her body tremble.

"No. I mean it," she gasped. "Stop." She elbowed him in the gut as she scrambled away, sitting up on her side of the bed.

"What the fuck?" His dick throbbed, angry and aching from being robbed of his release.

"Yeah, what the fuck? I said no sex. What do you think you're doing?"

"What am doing? Don't give me that shit. You were into it."

"I was sleeping."

"So the fuck was I when I started."

"But you woke and kept going."

"It's not the first time." He'd woken her with his cock more times than he could count.

"I wasn't mad at you the other times."

"Mad at me?" He had no idea what… "Oh, yeah. That." It was so fucking stupid.

"Yeah, that." She pulled up her shorts and got out of

bed.

"Come on, Alison. Lay down."

"No. I can't stay here because obviously you don't understand what no sex means."

"I was sleeping." His jaw clenched. He wasn't going to have any teeth left by the time she had their kid if this kept up.

"And you should've stopped when you woke."

"I would have if you hadn't been moaning and rubbing your ass against my cock."

"Don't blame this on me. " She stormed across the room.

"Fuck this, Alison. You wanted it as much as I did."

"But I don't now."

"Liar. Your pussy is screaming at you. It wants my cock." Just like his dick was raging at him to grab her and make her want him.

"It'll survive."

"I hope so because even if you come back and beg me, you're not getting any tonight."

"Nice try but I'm not stupid." She sent him a withering look.

"Worth a shot." He shrugged. "You're very competitive."

"Go to hell, Harker."

"Oh, I'm there." He grabbed his dick in his hand and started stroking. "Masturbatory hell."

"Have fun."

"You too and just so you know...I can hear your

vibrator."

"You can what?" Her face paled.

"Yep. I can't tell you how many nights I spent in here listening to you and that little toy. Hearing your soft gasps and moans, wondering what would happen if I walked into your room." He continued to stroke his cock. "You alone. So needy. So horny."

Her eyes dropped to his dick.

"Would you be happy to see me? Happy to let me touch you. Kiss you. Fuck you." He patted the bed. "Come here, Alison. You know you want to. You can be mad at me later."

She pulled her eyes away from his cock. "Go to hell, Harker." She turned and fled.

"I told you. I'm already there. Dick in my hand and everything," he shouted after her. He fucking hated jerking off.

CHAPTER 32: HARKER

The next day when Harker stepped into Alison's office it was like a punch in the stomach. She and Mac sat next to each other, heads close and talking in what may as well be robot-speak as far as he understood.

She glanced up at him, the happiness on her face turning quickly to irritation. She grabbed her phone from her pocket.

"Alison…"

His phone beeped. She stared at him expectantly.

"I'm not looking at my ph…"

Her eyes widened. It'd be just like her to use this ruse to win the damn bet.

"Dinner?" he asked.

She shook her head and typed something into the phone.

When the next message beeped, he did look at it.

ALISON: I'm not hungry. Busy working.

He started to text and then stopped. "Damn it. Have

dinner with me."

Mac stood and walked toward the door.

"Where are you going?" she asked.

Mac stopped, glancing from one to the other. "Ah..uhm..bathroom." He hurried past Harker and out of the room.

"I told you he was smart," he joked, hoping to lighten the mood.

"Go away." She turned back toward the computer, dismissing him.

"Come on. You like Mac. This is all working out."

"Go to hell."

"I told you. I'm already there."

"That's right. Masturbatory hell." Her eyes dropped to his crotch. "You should go somewhere private."

"Right now, I'm in regular hell because you've been avoiding me." He paused, his anger slipping away. "I miss talking to you. I think we should stop playing this game."

"You concede?" She stared at him a challenge in her eyes. "I didn't think you were a quitter."

"I'm not quitting. We'll call it a draw."

"No. I still plan on winning." She winced. "Shit."

"Don't worry. That wasn't today's phrase."

"Good. Now go away."

"You need to eat." He walked over to her and squatted. "You could be carrying my child." He put his hand on her stomach, needing to touch her somewhere, anywhere. "Please Alison, I miss you."

She frowned at him. "I have work to do. I'll be home

later." But she put her hand over his and didn't push him away.

"How much later? I'll order something. Or cook. You need to eat. You already skipped lunch—"

"I ate lunch."

"You did?" They always had lunch together, but today she hadn't come to his office.

"I had lunch with my new employee."

He hated how fucking pleased she was about that.

"Did you have something for lunch?" she asked.

He wanted to fist pump and shout hallelujah because the smugness in her expression changed to concern. He hadn't realized how much he missed someone caring about him.

"I know you get busy and forget but you need to eat."

"No, I didn't." He'd had a bagel around ten in the morning, but he hadn't technically eaten lunch. "I forgot. Usually you remind me but it's okay." He tried to look as pathetic as possible. "I can wait for dinner. Whenever you have time is fine."

She sighed as she brushed a strand of hair off his forehead. "No, we'll go have dinner, but this doesn't mean that I forgive you."

"Got it." He stood, taking her hand in his and pulling her to her feet.

"And this doesn't mean that we're having sex tonight either."

"Understood." Oh, they were so having sex tonight. She'd let him touch her and that meant he'd get around those bases and make it home at least one time tonight.

CHAPTER 33: ALISON

Alison let Harker lead her to the couch.

"Sit and I'll get you something to drink." He dropped her hand and headed toward the bar.

"I might be pregnant, remember?" She wasn't going to make this easy for him. If she did, he'd get suspicious, and she couldn't have that. She was going to win this damn game.

"True but one glass of wine this early in your pregnancy won't hurt." His eyes roamed over her and they were warm and filled with heat. "Do you think you're pregnant?"

"You know it's possible, but I doubt it. I don't feel any differently but bring me a water just in case."

He nodded and walked into the kitchen. "What do you want for dinner?" He came back out and sat next to her, putting the water on the coffee table.

"How about Indian food?"

"Sure." He pulled his phone from his pocket. "Let me find the number to one that's nearby."

"I expected you to argue." She frowned at him. "You

don't like Indian food."

"I don't but if it'll make you happy then I can eat it."
He glanced at her, not touching his phone.

The jerk was waiting for her to suggest that they get
something that he liked. Well, too bad. "Good. It will make
me happy. I like Indian food. I never eat it because you
don't like it but tonight…that will make me happier."

His eyes narrowed before he looked back at his phone,
tapping the screen and raising it to his ear. "Hello. Yes.
Hold on." He handed her the phone. "You should order. I
have no idea what you like."

"No, you don't."

"I meant regarding Indian food." By his tone he was
struggling to keep his temper in check. "I know exactly
what you like in other aspects of our life."

Her cheeks heated as his gaze roamed over her body.
That was no lie. She cleared her throat and ordered their
food.

CHAPTER 34: HARKER

"Thank you again for ordering me the chicken." Harker closed his takeout box.

"You mean the chicken nuggets." Alison handed him her empty container.

"Chicken fingers." He walked into the kitchen and tossed the boxes.

"Hmm. They looked like nuggets to me. You know, stuff a kid would eat."

"Adults like chicken nug...fingers too." He went back into the living room. Dinner was done, it was time for sex.

"I suppose." She stood. "I'm going to take a shower and go to bed."

"Great. I'll—"

"Alone."

"Alison, come on. Forgive me. Please." He was not above begging.

"I will." She gave him a quick kiss on his cheek. "Just not yet."

"When?" He captured her hand. "Later tonight?"

"Good night, Harker." She laughed, pulling from his

grasp.

"Night, Alison."

She stopped, turning toward him. "Why do you do that?"

"Do what?" Fuck, what had he done now?

"Answer like that?"

"Like what?" Maybe getting laid on a regular basis made her crazy because he swore, she'd never acted like this before they'd married.

"I say good night and you reply night.'

"Yeah, So. It's the same thing."

"It is not. I wish you a good night. A GOOD night. You know a happy one with—"

"If you really wanted me to have a good night, you'd let me shower with you."

Her eyes narrowed but she rambled on as if he hadn't spoken. "A night with good dreams and pleasant sleep but you wish me a night. What does that even mean? We both know it's night. And you do the same thing in the morning." She lowered her voice to imitate his. "Morning, Alison." She went back to her normal tone. "I know it's morning, but would it kill you to wish me a good morning or happy morning?"

"No one says happy morning." Why had he been upset when she hadn't been talking to him? It seemed like heaven now.

"That's not the point."

"For fuck's sake. What is the point? There is none, but if it'll make you happy, good"—he stressed the word—

"night, Alison."

"Ding. Ding. Ding. A point for me and that means, I win." She grinned from ear-to-ear.

He'd never wanted to strangle someone as badly as he did right now.

CHAPTER 35: HARKER

The next morning, Harker dried off after his shower and walked into the bedroom. It was Saturday but he had an early conference call and then he had to go look at a facility with Tobias.

Alison was still sleeping, curled on her side as far away from his spot on the bed as possible. Last night had been the second night in a row that they hadn't had sex. He pulled on his underwear and grabbed a pair of black slacks. He paused, staring at the jeans next to them. It was Saturday, the jeans were comfortable and most important Alison really liked it when he wore them.

He dropped the slacks and put on the jeans. He needed all the help he could get. He'd behaved like an ass last night. He still couldn't believe that she'd won the bet. He'd been so pissed that he'd hadn't even tried to have sex with her.

"Tried? Ha," he muttered to himself, as he walked to the closet to grab a business shirt. It wouldn't have taken much trying on his part. She'd been so happy with herself she would've jumped him if he'd given her half a chance.

Instead, he'd acted like a dumbass. As soon as she'd said ding-ding-ding—and he'd picked his jaw up off the floor—he'd gone into his office and had stayed there until late that night.

When he'd finally gone to bed, she'd been asleep with a smile on her fucking face, and he'd still wanted to throttle her. He hadn't been bested in anything in years.

He smirked slightly as he sat on the edge of the bed and put on his socks and shoes. He should've anticipated this. She was competitive and the smartest person he knew. Their kid was going to be out of this world intelligent. Of course, they wouldn't have a kid if they kept fighting.

"Harker? Where are you going?" she asked as she rolled onto her back.

He turned and his dick began to harden. Her hair was tangled, and her face was soft with sleep. He wanted to crawl back into bed and hold her. Okay. He'd fuck her first and then hold her, but unfortunately, neither of those things were going to happen. "I have that conference call and then I'm going to check out a facility with Tobias."

"Oh, yeah." She smiled slightly. "I forgot."

"I bet." He finished tying his shoe and then leaned across the bed toward her. "You were probably too busy planning your next move to pay any attention to what I said...unless it was goodnight, Alison."

She laughed. "That's true. I was."

"Well, congratulations." He kissed her softly. "I should've said that last night."

"Yes, you should've." She ran her hands up his chest

and over his shoulders before looping them around his neck. "You're a terrible loser. You need to work on that. It's not something you want our child to learn."

"If our child learns how to always win, he or she won't have to learn how to be a generous loser." He kissed her again. "Like me."

"Like you?"

"Yep. Like me." He kissed her once more, but this time his hands slid up to her breasts, his dick getting harder as her nipples pebbled beneath his palms.

"You are not a generous loser."

"Not that part." He tugged her T-shirt down. "The always winning part." He kissed her breast, teasing her nipple with his tongue.

"You lost last night." Her fingers played in his hair.

"I did." He gave her nipple one last tug with his teeth before leaning up and kissing her. "Especially when I didn't celebrate your victory with you."

"That was mean of you but"—she grinned—"when you stormed off to your office it did make winning a little more fun."

"You, my dear, are not a good winner." He laughed.

"Our child is doomed."

"I think so." He touched her cheek. "Seriously though, I haven't lost at anything in years, lots of years, but you...you did good." He kissed her again. "I wish I could stay here and celebrate with you, but I do have to go."

"Thank you." Her grin spread across her face and it made him happy in ways he didn't want to think about.

"You should've woken me last night and congratulated me." She rolled to his side of the bed and grabbed his pillow.

"I should've." He took in the sight of her snuggling his pillow and his stomach flipped. He was falling fast, and he had no idea how to slow things down or if he even wanted to.

"What?" She gave him a funny look. "Do you not want me to touch your pillow?" She started to sit up.

"No. That's not…Go ahead. I don't mind."

"Are you sure?" She dropped it.

"I'm sure." He walked over to her and handed her his pillow. "I liked it. That's all."

"You liked it?" Her eyes grew softer and filled with something that sent the fear of God into every cell in his body.

"Yeah, as long as you aren't wearing that vanilla perfume that makes everything smell like a bakery." He shivered in jest.

"You know, your child is going to want cookies." She hugged his pillow again.

"He or she can have cookies. They sell great ones in the stores." He headed for the door.

"That's not the same as homemade," she hollered after him.

"Nope. They're better. They don't make the house smell like vanilla."

CHAPTER 36: HARKER

Harker parked his car in the garage and got out. Today had been a long day. The conference call had been a waste of time and the facility had been a dump. The realtor had taken them to see three others and they'd all been in poor shape or outrageously expensive. All he wanted to do was go inside and see Alison. His night was planned. They'd have dinner, shower and fuck. He stepped inside the house and the scent of freshly baked cookies slapped him in the face.

"What the fuck," he muttered before he yelled, "Alison."

"Harker," she yelled back.

He couldn't help but chuckle. She normally just came running. He stepped into the kitchen and it looked like a cookie factory had exploded. "What the hell did you do?"

She pulled a pan from the oven, put it on the top of the stove and then turned. Her eyes were bright and her smile wide and excited. "I made you cookies. I got my mom's recipes. I didn't know which you'd like so I made sugar cookies, peanut butter and chocolate chip."

His day had just gone from bad to horrible. All those feelings of being treated like a piece of trash that no one wanted roared through him. He turned and went directly to the bar in the living room. He poured himself a few fingers of bourbon and tossed it back.

"Harker, is everything okay." She stood in the doorway looking unsure.

"No." He poured himself another drink. "Why would you do this? I told you I hate that smell."

"I thought that since I made them for you it'd make it better. You know, help to get rid of the bad memories by replacing them with good ones."

"It doesn't. It just brings the bad memories back."

"I'm sorry. I'll get rid of them."

"Why bother? You can't remove the smell." He was a kid again, those delicious scents filling his head and breaking his heart, reminding him of how unwanted and unloved he was. How alone he was. "This is why I don't talk about my past. People like you think you can fix it with some stupid gesture, but you can't."

"I'm sorry," she repeated. "I made a mistake but that's no reason to not talk about your past. Talking about it helps sometimes."

"Ah, that's right. The bet."

"This isn't about the bet."

"Isn't it?"

"No. Making the cookies had nothing to do with that."

"But you still want to know about my past, don't you? Even though you know I hate talking about it."

She hesitated but finally said, "Yes."

"Then let's get it over with so I can forget about it again. But this is it. You won the bet and I'll answer your questions but after tonight don't bring any of it up again. Ever. Understand?"

She nodded.

"Good." He started for the couch and stopped, grabbing the bottle of bourbon. He'd need it because Alison was tenaciously curious. He'd rather have her pull shrapnel from his gut with tweezers than have her dig into his past.

CHAPTER 37: ALISON

Alison sat on the chair across from Harker. She'd made a huge mistake. She'd thought he'd like the cookies but now they were fighting again and this time it was her fault. "I think we should stop the contest. We're both too competitive."

"I agree." He seemed to almost melt into the couch.

"Good and if I ask any questions that you really don't want to answer just tell me."

"What? You said we were done with our game."

"We are, but I did win." She hadn't even considered not asking him about his past. "And I need to know more about you for our child." But that was only part of the reason. She wanted to know everything about him for herself too.

"Our child doesn't need to know anything about my past," he almost growled.

"You don't think he or she might want to know why Dad gets mad when he smells baked goods?"

"No, I don't. It'll be one of my endearing quirks."

She bit her lip to stop from laughing. "Yes, but I still

think little junior might be curious."

"Junior will get over it but if you're collecting on your win then we're not stopping our game. I will win next week."

"You want to fight and not talk to each other for another week? Because I don't."

His frown deepened and he took a sip of his drink. "No, but if I agree to stop playing, we're going to La Petite Mort Club next Saturday."

"Okay." Her blood heated at the thought of what he might ask her to do.

His mouth opened and shut as if he'd been prepared to argue. "Good. And you agree to try whatever I want. We don't have to continue, but you agree to try it, right?" His dark eyes roamed over her.

"Yes." Her body, already at a slow simmer, started to bubble.

"Then fire away with your questions, but why don't you come over here" He patted the couch. "I may need a hug or something."

"Oh, that's so not a good idea." She laughed.

"I think it's an excellent idea. I'll need you to comfort me."

"I think I should ask the questions from here." She wanted to snuggle against his side and feel his large chest move as he breathed but if she got that close to him, they wouldn't be talking. She tucked her feet under her, making her less likely to move over by him.

"I think you'd be more comfortable right here." He

patted the couch again.

"I don't think comfortable is the right word for how I'll feel sitting next to you."

"Oh, come on. I'll behave, but I want you close when you make me relive all those horrible experiences from my childhood."

"Don't even try to make me feel bad about this. I won. You lost. If you'd won, you wouldn't change what you had planned."

"We'd both want to do what I picked. I don't want to do this."

"Too bad. It'll be good for you. Tell me about your childhood."

"Fine. I lived with my mom until I was eight when she OD'd. I never knew my dad. After that I spent the next ten years in different foster homes. I went to college—"

"Stop. You're listing facts. I know all that. It's in almost every article written about you. I want more than that."

"That's my childhood. My life. What else do you want me to say?"

"I want you to tell me about how this poor little boy became the man I see before me today. Confident. Successful. Driven."

"I don't know." He took another drink. "I guess, my life changed when I met Merri. I was in junior high and already on my way to trouble. I was running drugs and barely even going to class." His face softened. "Until she transferred into my school. She looked like an angel on the

outside but damn she was mean and prickly on the inside."
He smiled softly. "I'd never met anyone like her and for me
it was love at first smackdown."

"First smackdown?" She tried not to be jealous. She
was glad he'd found Merri but the look on his face made
Alison's gut churn with envy.

"Yeah. I thought I was so cool, but she was having
none of it. She wanted nothing to do with me and that made
me want her more."

"What happened? I know you went to college together.
Were the two of you dating?"

"No. Merri and I were just friends all through junior
high and high school. I was in love with her, but she dated
this guy, Pete, until we graduated. College was my chance
to move out of the friend-zone, but she fell hard for my
roommate Tobias."

"Oh, I'm so sorry. That must've broken your heart."
She felt bad for teenage Harker, but she was also happy
because if he and Merri had dated, they'd probably be
married now.

"Yeah but"—he tossed back his drink—"if it weren't
for her I'd probably be dead or in jail by now."

"No, you'd probably be some mafia or drug kingpin."

"Maybe." He chuckled as he refilled his glass.

"How did she help you to change?"

He sipped his drink, his eyes lost in the past. "She
wouldn't have anything to do with me the way I was, so I
changed."

"Why?" Only women who looked like Merri had the

ability to make men want to change, to become better. She'd seen it her entire life and she'd always been both fascinated and envious of their magic.

"Because even though she berated me and wouldn't date me she'd share her lunch with me, and she stuck up for me with the teachers. She was the first person who ever had my back."

"The teachers?"

"A lot of them had already written me off as not worth their time. The area was poor. I wasn't the first lost cause they'd seen."

"That's horrible."

"I don't blame them. I seldom showed up for class and if I was there, I wasn't doing anything but disturbing everyone else." He finished his drink and put the glass down on the end table before standing. "That's it. That's my childhood. Let's go to bed."

"Oh, no. We're not even close to done."

"But that's it. We went to college. We started the company. Merri and Tobias got married. We all stayed friends. We hired you and you know the rest." He held out his hand. "Come. I want to shower, and I need someone to wash my back."

The idea of that strong, muscular body under her hands, slippery and hot made her almost jump from the couch and drag him into the bathroom. The only thing stopping her was that she couldn't let this opportunity slip away. He'd never let it happen again. "No. That's not it." She leaned forward and refilled his glass. "Sit."

"What else do you want to know? I've told you everything."

"I want to know about your family."

"I have no family."

"That's a lie. I looked you up."

"Really? When?" He sounded flattered. "Before or after we got married?"

"Before. I wanted to know what kind of man and company I was going to be working for."

"Oh." He sat. "What do you want to know? There isn't much to tell."

"You have an aunt and uncle and they both have kids. Do you ever see them? Talk to them?

"Nope." His face tightened and he tossed back his drink and refilled it.

"Why not? Family can be a pain. I know. Years ago, my mom and aunt didn't get along very well. Aunt Tiff is kind of wild and my mom is…well, not wild."

"My family didn't want me when I was eight. I certainly don't need them now."

"How do you know they didn't want you? Sometimes, other things happen and—"

"I was in foster care for ten years, if they'd wanted me, they could've taken me."

"Maybe they didn't know. Was your mother estranged from her family?"

"Don't try and make them better than they are," he snapped. "You want to know why I hate my name?" His eyes met hers and they were filled with pain.

"Yes." But she wasn't sure she did. She'd seen him angry before but nothing like this. He was hurt and broken and filled with hate.

"My mother loved her brother. Adored him. She was always bragging about her brother in the military. She even named me after him."

"I thought his name was Gerry?"

"Augustus Gerald Harker, just like me. Even if he didn't want me, he should've taken me in for her but instead he used his military career as an excuse to leave me in foster care. He had a wife, but he claimed that they moved too much. It wasn't good for a child. It was bullshit. I lived in eight different foster homes in ten years. But my aunt"—he stared at the liquor in his glass—"this one is even better than my uncle's lie. She wouldn't take me because she didn't want me to corrupt her kids." He looked up at her and his eyes were haunted and filled with pain. "I was eight years old. How in the hell could I corrupt anyone? I was just a kid."

CHAPTER 38: ALISON

"They were wrong." So freaking wrong. Alison didn't remember moving but she must've because she now sat on the couch her hand resting on Harker's arm. "They should've come for you."

His eyes glistened as he slowly leaned toward her. Her heart thudded at his uncertainty. This wasn't like him. If he wanted something he took it. She'd never known him to hesitate about anything until now. She grabbed his shirt, yanked him to her and kissed him.

He captured her head in his hands, holding her as he took over the kiss. It was raw and wild, filled with desperation fueled by pain. She couldn't fix his past, but she could let him know that now he was wanted, loved. She froze for a second. Loved? Did she love him?

He noticed her hesitation and broke the kiss, his dark eyes searching hers. This wasn't the time to worry about her heart. It was time to help heal his. She leaned forward and kissed him again as she untucked his shirt, sliding her hands underneath and running them up his chest.

His tongue thrust into her mouth as he lifted her onto

his lap. She spread her legs, straddling him. His kisses slowed, becoming more coaxing than demanding, letting her set the pace as she rocked against him.

She tugged at his shirt and he lifted his arms. Buttons popped as she yanked it over his head. She needed him naked. She ran her fingernails up and down his chest, loving how his breathing increased and his dick grew harder beneath her.

"Take off your shirt," he ordered.

She lifted it slowly, teasing him as her pussy throbbed from the heat in his gaze. The uncertainty was gone, replaced by desire. She pulled her shirt off over her head and reached behind her. The motion pushing her chest closer to his face. His hot breath whispered across her skin as she unfastened her bra and let it slide down her arms, baring her breasts.

"You're so fucking beautiful."

"So are you." She touched his cheek, and he lifted his gaze to hers. "Inside and out." She kissed him softly, her hand sliding between them to stroke his cock.

He grabbed her ass, pulling her harder against his erection but she shifted away, kissing along his cheek and neck before moving down his chest. She slid off his lap to the floor. Her mouth trailed along his abdomen, his muscles trembling under her lips and tongue. He was hard and ready, but she was going to make him forget everything. His past didn't matter. Nothing mattered except right now. She kissed along the ridge in his pants, biting gently.

He grunted, spreading his legs and watching her like a

king watches his subject but she didn't care. He was her king, and she was going to worship him.

CHAPTER 39: HARKER

Harker watched as Alison unfastened his pants. He gathered her hair, holding it away so he could see her face. She slid her hand inside his underwear, stroking his cock.

"Take off my pants." He didn't want anything between them. He lifted, letting her pull his jeans down to his knees. She removed his shoes and socks, kissing his feet. His leg twitched when her tongue tickled along the sole of his foot.

"You're ticklish." She smiled up at him. "I'll have to remember that."

"I think I'm in trouble."

"Oh, you are." She laughed as she removed his pants and underwear, tossing them to the side. "But later. Right now…" She lifted onto her knees, her eyes heating at the sight of his cock.

His nostrils flared and his dick must've grown another inch as she licked her lips. There was nothing better in this world than a woman who loved sucking cock. They couldn't fake that look of eagerness. He moaned as her hand wrapped around his shaft and she slowly licked up his length.

"Look at me." His voice was gruff. He needed to see that spark of desire in her eyes as she sucked his dick.

Her gaze met his—amused, eager, hot as hell—as she teased her tongue around his tip. The sensation made his balls tighten and his eyes drift half-closed. He inhaled sharply as she took him into her mouth and sucked. It was heaven—hot, wet, tight heaven. She sucked harder and his fingers dug into the couch cushion. His other hand tightened in her hair as his hips thrust into her mouth. She didn't hesitate. She opened wider, taking him deep and letting him push into her throat.

He should stop, slow down but his body bucked as his hand held her in place. Her eyes watered and she tried to swallow, the pressure squeezing his dick. Her gag reflex kicked it, tightening on his cock. He dropped his hold, letting her pull off him. She inhaled deeply, her eyes watering.

"You okay?" He touched her cheek gently.

She nodded, her breathing getting easier. She wiped her lips rubbing the spit on his cock before taking him into her mouth again. This time she guided him into her throat, lowering her head until she had almost all of him inside her.

He groaned. Her throat was so fucking tight, squeezing his dick in the most exquisite way. His head dropped back onto his shoulders as she played with his nuts while she bobbed up and down on his dick.

"Fuck. I'm gonna come." His fingers tangled in her hair, pulling her off his cock. She gazed up at him, confused.

"I want to be inside you." He needed to feel her come on his cock. He needed to make her his.

"Okay." She stood, shimmying out of her pants and underwear. She put her hands on his shoulders to straddle him.

"No. The other way. Turn around." He grabbed her waist, turning her before pulling her down toward his lap. "Spread your legs." She obeyed without hesitation and he slid the tip of his cock inside her. "Now. Come here." He guided her lower as he thrust upward, pushing all the way inside of her.

"Ah…god…Harker." Her body stiffened and he stilled, letting her get used to his size. "You feel so much bigger like this."

He grabbed her throat, pulling her back against his chest so her head rested alongside his. "Good, huh?" He needed to fuck, to come but she had to be ready first.

"Yes. Really good." She tightened her inner muscles and he moaned.

"Ride me hard then, baby. Ride me hard."

CHAPTER 40: ALISON

Alison lifted and lowered herself, Harker's long, hard dick sliding in and out, stretching her.

"Find your rhythm." Harker's hands slipped upward, cupping her breasts.

"How's that?" She rocked up and down on his length. It felt good but not great.

"You tell me." He pinched her nipples and her back arched, pushing his dick against her G-spot. Her eyes closed as she moaned. "Oh…yeah…Do that again."

"My pleasure." He kissed her neck while he played with her nipples.

That felt good but it wasn't what she'd meant. So, she changed her motion. Instead of moving up and down she rocked back and forth like she was riding a horse and every time she rolled forward his dick rubbed against her G-spot. Sparks sizzled through her body as her pace increased. She added a wiggle, bearing down on his dick and pushing it against that spongy bundle of nerves. She clutched at his arms, her body rocking faster and faster as pleasure pulsed through her.

"That's it, baby. Take it. Use me. Use my cock."

His words raw and gruff pushed through her haze of desire. She turned her head, her lips against his. "Never. I'd never use you." She'd only love him. Her body stilled as the truth of that thought filled her. She didn't want to love him. It wasn't safe. This was temporary.

"Keep going. It's okay." He grabbed her hips moving to the rhythm she'd set before, his dick stroking against her G-spot with each long, hard thrust.

She clung to his arms. Her fear pushed aside by pleasure. She rocked back and forth as he pushed into her. The dual movements making his cock hit that spot harder and harder until she couldn't take anymore, and she shattered.

CHAPTER 41: HARKER

Harker needed to come, but this position wasn't doing it for him. It was good for a slow fuck but that was over. He lifted Alison off his dick and lowered her to the couch.

"Get on your hands and knees." He knelt behind her and grabbed his cock, sliding back inside her. Her slick, wet heat wrapped around his dick, squeezing him. He grabbed her hips, holding her in place as he thrust into her hard and fast. She squeaked, tiny little sounds of pleasure that drove him mad and he fucked her faster. His nuts tightening preparing to explode.

"I'm going to make you come again."

"Harker, I...I can't," she panted.

He slapped her ass. "You will." He let go of her hip with one hand and slid it around her side and between her legs, searching through her slick wetness for her clit. He rubbed her hard, little nub mercilessly as he fucked her.

"Oh...god...oh...please." She was ready to come again. Her body tightening even more around his cock.

"That's it." He pressed down on her clit, pumping into her hard and fast and she bucked under him.

"Oh…oh…god…Harker." Her arms trembled as her fingers scraped at the sofa, her body thrusting frantically against his, lost in desire.

He thrust into her one more time and came as she broke apart beneath him. He collapsed on top of her, surrounding her, claiming her as his. He didn't want to ever move again.

CHAPTER 42: HARKER

Harker lay in bed, Alison tucked against his side. After the couch he'd carried her to their room and had crawled into bed. He wasn't sleepy. Usually if he wasn't tired, he was working or fucking but right now he was content to hold her in silence and enjoy being with her.

"Harker?"

"Yes." He sighed. So much for silence.

"I'm sorry I asked about your family. Actually"—she moved so she lay on his chest her hands under her chin—"I'm not sorry that I asked and I'm glad you told me, but I am sorry that your childhood was terrible. That your family sucks."

"Thank you but it was a long time ago. It doesn't matter anymore." Damn, this woman made him warm inside.

"It does matter. Things like that…things that happen when we're kids make a big difference in the rest of our lives."

"I got over it."

"I don't think you have." The intensity of her gaze

made him want to squirm away from her.

"Believe me. I have."

"Have you talked to them? What about your grandparents? You didn't mention them."

"My grandpa had Alzheimer's and my grandma didn't want the added burden of a troubled kid." He was glad the words came out as if they still didn't eat a hole through him like acid.

"Oh. I'm sorry about your granddad and I can understand why your grandma didn't take you in. She probably thought—"

"You can?" He'd expected her to be on his side.

"My dad had cancer and it was all we could do to stay afloat. I don't mean money; I mean emotionally. Me and my mom…Sometime there's only so much you can take."

"I was her grandchild. The child of her daughter who'd just died."

"And she should've taken you in"—her fingers caressed his chest—"but I'm saying it's hard and we're all human. She may not have been as strong as you or maybe she thought her other kids would..." Her eyes narrowed. "How do you know all this. There's no way child services told you."

"I paid for my records. All of them." It was the first thing he'd done once he'd become rich.

"They aren't supposed to do that."

"Money can buy everything."

"That's not true. It doesn't buy what's important."

"Really? Then why did my uncle and aunt contact me

once I became a billionaire?"

"Those bastards."

He almost flinched from the fire in her eyes.

"I hope you told them where they could go."

He loved her indignation and fury because it was for him. She was in his corner. He'd known the moment he'd met her that she'd be loyal and steadfast. She wouldn't be like everyone else and leave him when things went bad. "It doesn't matter." He rolled, pinning her beneath him.

"It does matter."

"No, it doesn't." He brushed the hair from her face. "Not anymore." Because he'd found her, and she was all that mattered now. He kissed her, telling her without words how he felt.

CHAPTER 43: HARKER

Harker paced in the living room, eager and yet nervous about tonight. Last week with Alison had been perfect. Without the game the two of them had spent the days and evenings together like before, talking and working but it was so much better. Instead of him stealing surreptitious glances at her and going to bed horny and alone, he'd seduce her or grab her and haul her to bed. Either way ended with him fucking her until he was too exhausted to move.

"Are you almost ready?" Harker couldn't believe he was as nervous as a schoolboy with his first girlfriend. He really wanted Alison to enjoy the night he'd planned for them at La Petite Mort Club.

"Almost. Stop barking at me," yelled Alison from the bedroom.

"Oh, you'd so better watch that mouth."

"Or what?" She laughed.

"Or I'll take exquisite pleasure in punishing you at the Club." He stopped near the doorway to their bedroom.

"You'll do that anyway."

"Normally I would but I have other things planned for tonight."

"Are you sure about this." The door opened and Alison stepped into the living room.

The blood fled his brain and went straight to his cock. Her hair hung loose, making his fingers twitch to grab it and guide her head down his chest. Her hair would be soft and fragrant, seducing him as she made her way to his dick.

Her lavender dress stopped at mid-thigh, displaying her firm, sexy legs and the scooped neckline accentuated her breasts, drawing his eyes. She must be wearing a pushup bra because her small mounds filled the top and made his mouth water.

"Is everything okay?" She glanced down at her outfit. "Should I change? I know—"

He swallowed, wetting his dry throat. "You look stunning." He walked over to her, drawn to her like a moth to a light.

"Are you sure? I know you wanted me to wear my wedding dress but—"

"I would've preferred that, but you look beautiful in this too." His thumb traced across the soft fabric, teasing her nipple. It'd only take a little push and her breast would be free, but if he started now, they'd never make it out of the house.

"That white dress would stand out at the Club like a pimple on your nose."

"I want you to stand out." He bent and kissed her, tugging slightly on her hardening nipple. "I want everyone to notice you because I want them all to know that you're mine."

"Oh, Harker." She kissed him quickly. "That's sweet but I don't think most people will care. I've seen the women there and...I'm not feeling sorry for myself, but they are way more attractive than I am."

"You underestimate your attraction." He forced himself to stop playing with her nipple before he carried her to their bedroom. "Most of the men at the Club prefer unique, intelligent females who understand what it is to be a woman."

"What does that even mean?" She raised her brow. "I have a funny feeling I'm about to be insulted."

"Not at all." He skimmed his fingers along the warm, soft skin of her throat because he couldn't stand so close and not touch her. "The best kind of woman understands that she doesn't need to eliminate what makes her female in her quest for feminism. I'm all for equal rights and feminism. Women are as smart as men, as hard working and should be compensated for that, but the woman who can work with men, compete with men and not eliminate the unique things that make men-men and women-women, is a female to be cherished above all others. She's a partner not a subordinate."

"So you don't want me to be your sub?" Her eyes sparkled mischievously.

"In the bedroom? Yes, I definitely do. In everyday life? No. I prefer a partner." His hand slid inside the top of her dress, caressing her breast.

"If you don't stop that we'll never make it out of here." Her voice was breathless as she arched her back slightly, pushing more firmly into his hand.

"That'd be a shame. I have so much to show you tonight." He pinched her nipple, making her sigh before he removed his hand from her dress. "Come. It's time to go play."

CHAPTER 44: ALISON

Alison tried not to dig her nails into Harker's arm as he led her to a couch toward the back of the Club. They'd discussed what he wanted to do tonight, and even though she'd agreed she wasn't so sure it was a good idea. She sat as Harker ordered their drinks.

"Ethan will be here shortly." He sat next to her, his hand resting on her thigh.

"Are you sure about this?" She wasn't. It was tempting and exciting but if it were another woman joining them, she'd be jealous.

"Have you changed your mind?" His dark eyes didn't give her any clue as to what he wanted.

"I...I don't know."

"You can stop at any time." He touched her cheek. "If you don't want to do this, that's fine too."

"I...Do you want to do this?" It was a silly question because he'd arranged it, but she couldn't comprehend how he'd be okay with watching another man touch her, kiss her.

His eyes searched hers. "This is about me helping you

to experience things you've only fantasized about."

"And you'll be okay with this…with seeing me with another man?"

"Yes. I want to be the one to show you these new levels of pleasure." He kissed her softly.

"But it doesn't make sense." She turned toward him. "You're okay with this but the contract says we're to be monogamous. This is not monogamy. This is polyandry."

"No, it's not." He smiled at her. "Ethan isn't your second husband, and he's not going to fuck you." His hand cupped her breast, squeezing gently. "The only one fucking you tonight will be me."

"Oh. Okay. I understand." She smiled, but she wanted to cry. She was in love with him, and he thought of her as his student. If he wasn't concerned about paternity, he'd be okay with her fucking another man while he watched.

"I'm not sure you do." His brow wrinkled with concern.

"Hello." Ethan's whiskey smooth voice interrupted their conversation and Alison couldn't stop her body from responding. He was the hottest man she'd ever seen. He smelled sexy, he looked sexy, his voice made her insides melt and she was going to be his plaything tonight.

CHAPTER 45: HARKER

"May I join you?" Ethan motioned to the spot on the couch next to Alison.

"Ah..." Alison cleared her throat, a faint blush coloring her cheeks. "Sure."

"Thank you." Ethan sat.

Usually Harker admired the other man's obsession with asking permission for everything, but tonight it was a little irritating. They all knew what was going to happen. They'd planned everything in advance. Soon, Ethan would be touching her, restraining her, eating her pussy. The man didn't need to ask if he could sit next to her on the freaking couch and there was definitely no reason for Alison to almost fucking melt when she looked at the other man. Yes, women found Ethan gorgeous, but he was just a man.

"What do you like to drink?" Ethan stared at Alison as if she were the last woman in the world.

Harker could swear the other man was fluttering his lashes at her from the way she was blushing.

"Ah…I drink a lot of different things. Wine, tequila, whisky, beer."

"Do you like cognac?" Ethan brushed a bit of hair from Alison's shoulder and Harker was sure she sighed.

"I've never tried it."

"Perfect because tonight is the night for trying new things." Ethan raised his hand and a waitress appeared as if by magic. The service here was always good but that was almost unworldly. "Please bring us the bottle of Remy Martin Cognac Louis XIII. I left it with Bea behind the bar."

"Yes, sir." The waitress left.

"That's a twenty-five-thousand-dollar bottle of cognac." Harker was rich but he never wasted his money on anything so frivolous.

"Twenty-five thousand dollars?" Alison's face paled and she almost choked.

"It's on me." Ethan's hand brushed Alison's arm as if by accident but Harker knew better. "Tonight the expense is worth it."

"I didn't say I wouldn't pay for it." Harker didn't want her to think he was cheap.

"I didn't say you did." Ethan gave him a confused look over Alison's head. "I've been waiting to have a drink from the bottle." He looked at Alison and although his smile was charming there was a hint of sadness to it. "You'd be doing me a favor. I bought it to share with a woman I'd been dating but we broke up. It just sits in my office reminding me of her."

"I'm so sorry." Alison touched Ethan's arm. "What happened? By the way you said that I'm guessing she dumped you." Her eyes widened in horror. "Oh. I shouldn't have said that. I'm sorry. I…" She glanced at Harker. "He can tell you. I talk a lot especially when I'm nervous and I never think before I speak. I don't have a filter or at least not a good one. The words just flow—"

"Please don't apologize." Ethan covered her small hand, which still rested on his arm, with his larger one. "I prefer candor"—his eyes took on a cloudy sadness that Harker could tell wasn't rehearsed—"and yes, she broke up with me."

That was the problem with Ethan. Everything about him was authentic. He fucked women right and left but they all adored him. He never lied to them or used them. He truly liked each and every one of them and it showed in his face. No wonder the fucker had them dropping at his feet and begging for a taste of his cock.

Harker may have arranged this evening, but it was time to remind them both that Alison belonged to him. He took her other hand and kissed it, before tucking it by his side. "Alison doesn't like cognac."

CHAPTER 46: ALISON

"Actually, I've never had it." She had no idea why Harker was being so rude. She turned back toward Ethan. "I'd love to try some."

Harker's grip on her hand tightened and he mumbled something.

She ignored him. She knew that grumble. He was being grumpy about something. "If you don't mind me asking, what happened with this woman? Were the two of you serious?" She couldn't imagine anyone breaking up with Ethan. He was charming, successful, rich and absolutely gorgeous.

"What I said"—interrupted Harker—"is that I don't like cognac."

"Okay. That's not a problem." Ethan waved over a waitress. "Bring a bottle of bourbon for Harker. Apparently, he's not in the mood for cognac."

"I'm never in the mood for cognac," he muttered.

"I've seen you drink it before," said Ethan.

"I must've been drunk."

"No. You weren't." Ethan gave him a funny look.

"I may not have been falling down but I had to have been pretty drunk to drink cognac."

Alison wasn't in the mood to listen to these two argue about alcohol. She shifted toward Ethan. "If you don't want to talk about what happened with this woman, I understand. I've had plenty of breakups. There was this one guy who stood me up so he could stay home and watch TV." She shook her head. "Who does that? I was going to put out that night too. I felt horrible and didn't want to tell anyone. I blamed myself but then I talked to Ellie. Of course, she and I have been friends for a long time and you and I…well, we've just met. But"—she touched Ethan's arm—"it's good to talk to somebody. It does make you feel better especially if you bash the person who broke up with you." She laughed. "Oh, we so bashed that guy and then there was this other guy who picked me up for a date and his mother was driving. I know. I know. You probably think I'm talking about junior high or something but I'm not. We were both in our twenties. He'd lost his license. I probably should've been understanding. None of us are perfect, but his mom went into the restaurant with us and everything." She shook her head, laughing. "I couldn't see him again. I just couldn't. Boy did Ellie and I laugh about that one." She sighed. "I know you men don't like to talk about feelings but…" She clamped her hand over her mouth at the horrified yet amused expression on Ethan's face. "Sorry," she mumbled around her fingers. "I told you I talk a lot."

"There is"—Ethan pried her fingers away from her face—"absolutely no reason to apologize. I find your chatter charming." He grinned and Alison almost melted onto the couch. "And funny."

"Just wait," muttered Harker. "The charm wears off."

Alison pulled her hand from Harker's grasp. She wanted to slap the big jerk but that'd make this even more awkward. So instead, she straightened the hem of her dress and folded her hands in her lap.

"I don't think it will." Ethan gave Harker an odd look before his beautiful blue eyes went back to her. His gaze was warm and interested. "I enjoy hearing people talk, especially women. They're a conundrum to me. No matter how much I try to understand them, they always surprise me." He smiled softly at her. "Plus, I don't talk to too many people, so this is certainly a welcome change."

The waitress came over with their drinks.

Ethan poured two glasses of cognac. "It's important to warm it a little but not too much or it'll destroy the flavor." He cupped the round snifter in his hands for a few minutes before handing it to her.

"I've never drank out of a glass like this." She held it between her hands like he had.

"That's part of what I love about cognac." Ethan swirled the liquid in his glass, his gaze intense.

Alison felt herself leaning toward him.

"The shape of the glass. The warmth from your hand, heating the alcohol." Ethan held it up to his nose. "The scents. A hint of orange. Caramel. The whole experience is sensual." His gaze met hers. "Here's to getting to know each other better." He tapped his glass against hers.

Alison's pulse raced and her body tingled but she wasn't sure she was ready for this. She glanced at Harker but that was like throwing gas on a fire. His eyes were almost black with desire. Her body gushed, leaving her panties damp. Only this man could do that to her with one look. She took a sip as she turned back to Ethan.

His eyes roamed unashamedly over her body, stopping on her breasts.

Her nipples tightened. Okay. Maybe she could do this. She took a gulp of her drink and then coughed. "Oh. It's a little stronger than I thought but sweet."

"Do you like it?" Ethan's gaze lifted to hers as he shifted a little closer, his hand resting on the couch next to her thigh.

She nodded but she was pretty sure she'd just made that cartoon gulp sound. She needed to slow this down because her nerves were on edge and her body was flushed. Or maybe she needed to speed this up. She wasn't sure what she should do so she did what she always did. "Why don't you talk to many people? I'd think working…owning this place you'd be talking to people all the time. I'm glad you enjoy people who talk a lot because I talk even more when I'm nervous. The more nervous I am the more the words spill from my mouth, and I have to say that I'm pretty darn nervous right now." She took a huge breath, preparing for the next burst of words.

"You're adorable." Ethan laughed.

Good lord, this man was even more attractive when he smiled like that. She literally fanned herself a couple of times before she realized what she was doing. Unfortunately, he didn't miss it because his smile widened.

"It's not funny." But she had to smile back at him because he was beautiful and genuine.

"It kind of is," said Ethan. "I've never seen a woman actually do that before."

"Really? I'm surprised. I bet a lot have wanted to around you."

"I don't know about that, but I know no one ever has." His grinned deepened. "You're my first."

"Oh, you are trouble." Her face heated. "No, you're the devil. Handsome, charming, and dangerous to a woman's virtue. Not that I still have my virtue. I lost that in the back of a Chevy…"

Ethan touched her cheek and kissed her. His lips were warm and firm, making her toes tingle. Unlike Harker's kisses which were hot and demanding, Ethan's was more permission than possession. She turned, glancing at Harker. Even though their marriage wasn't real, he was her husband and this man had just kissed her in front of him.

Harker's gaze was incinerating as he leaned closer. His large body engulfing hers as he captured her chin, holding her for his kiss. His tongue traced her lower lip, and she opened for him. He immediately deepened the kiss, exploring her mouth, possessing her and making her body burn. She grabbed his shirt to steady herself as her world spun into passion.

Ethan moved closer, his strong body warming her back as he pushed her hair out of his way. His other hand rested on her waist, as he nibbled his way along her neck. Her body throbbed with sensation as both men worshiped her. Harker's hand cupped her breast, teasing her nipple through the cloth and she moaned softly into his mouth. He nipped her lower lip as he pinched her nipple.

Ethan nibbled on her ear as his hand moved up from her waist, capturing her other breast. "Do you like this, Alison?"

She couldn't speak. She could barely think as Harker kissed her deeper. Feelings and sensations whirled inside her. She let go of Harker's shirt with one hand and put it over Ethan's on her breast. He stilled for a second as if waiting to see if she'd push him away, but she only held him closer.

"I'll take that as a yes." Ethan smiled against the side of her neck as he slid his hand inside her dress.

Her eyes closed as she arched her back, pressing her breast more firmly into his hand and he began to tease her nipple with slow circles of his thumb.

Harker broke from her mouth. He kissed his way down her throat toward her breasts, leaving a trail of heat and desire. She squeezed her legs together. She was wet and aching for him. Harker's lips skimmed across her chest, pushing Ethan's hand aside as he captured her nipple and sucked. Her head dropped back onto Ethan's shoulder as she moaned, her legs widening for him, waiting for him to possess her.

Ethan's hot breath tickled her ear as his hand slid slowly up and down her thigh, each trip pulling her skirt up more and more. His hand was rough and hot on her skin, making her burn and ache. His long fingers moved inward and upward, closer and closer to where she needed him to touch. Harker teased her nipple with his teeth and bit down. She gasped, her eyes flying open as pain and pleasure shot through her.

People stood around them, drinking and talking. Their eyes heavy-lidded with desire. A few men stroked themselves through their pants. She didn't want to do this in front of a crowd.

"What's the matter, Alison?" Ethan's hand rested on her upper thigh, only inches away from her pussy.

Harker continued sucking her nipple as his long fingers stroked between her legs, making her throb even more.

Her body quivered, but she grabbed his wrist, stopping him. "People are watching." She tugged on his hair with her other hand.

He pulled his mouth from her breast, his dark eyes burning as he gazed up at her. "What?" His voice was thick with lust.

"People are watching." She tucked her boob back into her dress.

"So?" Harker glanced to the side.

"S-so?" she sputtered.

"If you want to stop, use your safeword." He sat up, a hint of anger in his tone. "Because next time a tug on my hair isn't going to make me quit touching you."

"Perhaps we should take this to your room." Ethan stood, motioning for the waitress who stepped from the crowd.

She'd probably been watching. Alison wanted to crawl under the couch and hide.

"Good idea." Harker turned to the waitress. "Take our drinks to suite eleven."

The waitress gathered the drinks and was gone in a flash.

"Come." Harker stood, holding out his hand.

"She'll definitely do that. Several times." Ethan laughed as he led the way to the back of the Club.

CHAPTER 47: HARKER

Harker strode into their private suite at Le Petite Mort Club and headed straight to the bedroom. He was more than ready to continue where he, Ethan and Alison had left off.

"Wait," said Alison. "Maybe we should talk a little more."

"Why?" He stopped mid-stride. Talking was the last thing he wanted to do.

"Because the lady suggested it." Ethan sent him a disgusted look. "Please, Alison. Have a seat." He motioned to the couch.

His friend was right. She looked like she was ready to bolt out the door. Her eyes darted around the room and the beautiful flush on her cheeks and chest had faded. He knew he should slow down and seduce her into the bedroom, but his blood ran hot and he was desperate to claim her.

"So." Ethan sat on the couch, stretching his arm along the back, making a perfect place for Alison to sit. "How do you like being married to Harker?" He smirked.

"She likes it just fine." He walked across the room and

took Alison's hand, kissing it. "Don't you?"

"Of course." She smiled mischievously at him and his heart did a somersault. "Although he still orders me around all the time."

"But that's different when done in the bedroom, isn't it?" Ethan's gaze heated as it roamed over her in a slow caress.

"Yes." The word was a breathless whisper and her lovely blush returned.

Harker didn't like how her face had softened as she stared at Ethan. She needed to remember that she was his. His wife. The mother of his kids. Kid. Singular. He kissed her. His temper eased as she melted against him, her hands running up his chest and over his shoulders to tangle in his hair. He tipped his head, deepening the kiss as his hands slid down her back to her ass. He pulled her into him, letting her feel how hard he was for her before running his hands down her butt and back up, lifting the dress with them. He needed her naked. Needed to touch her soft, warm skin.

Ethan stepped behind her, kissing along her neck. Alison stiffened, making Harker want to grin, until her legs shook with need and he had to tighten his hold to keep her from crumbling to the floor. That mother fucker's lips were magic. He broke his kiss, moving down her neck and pushing the other man out of his way.

Ethan stepped back, kissing across her shoulders before his head disappeared behind her back. The straps of her dress loosened. The bastard was undressing her. Yes,

Harker wanted her naked, but he should be undressing her and exposing all her warm, smooth skin.

He kissed along her other shoulder, his hand squeezing her breast as he pulled her dress down. He nibbled her collar bone and along the top of her bra where her skin was especially fragrant from her perfume. He stepped back, watching as the dress slid down her body until only her heels and her lingerie remained.

Her bra was lavender with black lace, and it cupped and lifted her breasts until they almost spilled from the top. Her panties were the same color, the soft purple between her legs stained by her desire.

"You're fucking gorgeous. Every time I see those heels, I'm going to think of you like this."

Her gaze locked with his. "I guess I'll have to start wearing them to work."

"As long as you understand that it means I'm going to fuck you every time I catch you alone." He smirked.

She laughed and then her eyes widened as Ethan knelt behind her, his hands running up her legs to her ass.

CHAPTER 48: ALISON

Alison had forgotten about Ethan. She had no idea how that was even possible. The man was not forgettable, but she'd gotten so lost in the desire in Harker's eyes that everything but him and her had vanished.

She jumped as Ethan's hands cupped her butt, his hot breath blowing across her skin. She shivered, her gaze still locked with Harker's as Ethan kissed along the edge of her panties, his mouth hot and wet. She inhaled deeply and Harker's eyes dipped to her breasts before he stepped forward, capturing her face in his hands and kissing her. His kisses were usually aggressive but this one was almost punishing—his lips firm as he demanded her surrender. His tongue thrust into her mouth, claiming every inch as her body softened against his. Her pussy throbbed, aching and empty, needing him to touch her, kiss her, fill her.

Ethan pulled her panties down, squeezing her cheeks in his hands before his hot mouth trailed across them licking and nipping. Harker's hand cupped her breast, teasing her nipple as he kissed a path down her chest. Ethan's fingers skimmed up her body as he stood, lighting a fire with each touch. She was trapped between these two alpha males, their bodies hard and hot, pressing into her softness. Ethan unfastened her bra and Harker pulled it off.

She was naked in front of two men. She should be embarrassed but…Harker's mouth came down on her breast, sucking her nipple and she moaned. Her hands tangled in his hair and her head dropped back. Ethan turned her face, kissing her. His tongue sliding into her mouth, seducing her with his taste—sweet cognac and male. Harker moved away from her breast, grabbing her chin and turning her toward him. His kiss was hard and desperate, his hand on her ass, pulling her against him.

Ethan's lips trailed down her neck toward her breast. He blew across her hard nipple before teasing it with his tongue. She moaned into Harker's mouth, her back arching, pushing her breast toward Ethan. Harker nipped her lip and then his mouth was on her other breast, sucking hard. Her legs trembled and she grabbed the men's heads, clinging to them to keep from crumbling to the floor. Harker pushed Ethan's hand away before grabbing her other breast.

Ethan straightened, wrapping his arms around her waist, his large hands sliding down her thighs. "Open." His voice was gruff in her ear as he pulled her legs apart. She trembled as his hand slid between them, stroking along her wet, swollen flesh.

Harker lifted off her breast. He captured her mouth with his as he pulled her against him, the cool air on her back making her shiver before Harker's hand thrust between her legs, his thumb twirling over her clit.

"Maybe we should head to the bedroom." Ethan's voice was tense.

"Excellent idea." Harker grabbed her ass, lifting her. "Wrap your legs around my waist."

She obeyed without hesitation. She needed to feel him between her legs. She hooked her ankles around his back, sighing as his hard cock pressed against her pussy. He kissed her as he strode to the bedroom. She moaned against his lips as his fingers dug into her ass, holding her against him, his dick rubbing against her clit with each step.

He lowered her to the bed and followed her down. His kiss turned harder, more demanding and his hands were everywhere, teasing her breasts, slapping her thigh, sliding through her wetness and stroking between her legs. He kissed his way down her body, making her quiver in anticipation as his lips teased along her stomach and across her abdomen.

She glanced over his shoulder and the breath caught in her chest as Ethan stripped off his shirt. He was beyond gorgeous. Harker had a great body, but Ethan looked like a statue made from warm, living flesh.

Harker's tongue licked along her slit and she moaned. Her hands tangled in his thick, black hair, holding him close. Her back arched as he sucked her clit. She closed her eyes, lost in the pleasure of Harker's talented mouth and then Ethan was kissing her breast, tugging her nipple into his mouth. Sparks shot through her body from everywhere. It was so much. Too much as Harker slid a finger inside her and Ethan tugged on her nipple with his teeth. One of her hands went to Ethan's head, holding him close as the other grabbed the sheets. Harker thrust another finger inside her, his tongue and lips still working her clit. Her back arched, pressing herself closer to both men. Her body tightened, reaching for her release as Harker pumped into her, curling his fingers. Her hips thrust with his rhythm, rocking against his face. She was almost there. She just needed…He pulled his fingers from her.

"No. Please," she moaned.

CHAPTER 49: HARKER

Harker had never been so horny and angry at the same time in his life. Alison lay there with her freaking hand tangled in Ethan's hair. She should be clinging to him. He was the one eating her pussy and taking her to the edge of release not Ethan.

Ethan raised his head from her breast. "Time to switch places?"

Alison opened her eyes. They were dark with the desire that he'd created. Him. No one else.

"No. It's not time to switch places." He kissed her thigh. That pussy was his.

"Okay." Ethan rolled Alison to her side. "How about this. I get the back and you can have the front." His fingers slid between her legs.

"No." He grabbed Ethan's arm, jerking his hand away from her.

"What the fuck, Harker?" Ethan sat up. "We need to talk."

"We don't need to talk. Just hold her fucking hands." He might be able to stomach the other man touching them, but nothing else.

"Hold her hands? You invited me here to be a fucking rope?" Ethan got out of the bed and grabbed his shirt. "We need to talk now." He strode into the other room.

Harker followed, slamming the door behind him.

"What the hell is your problem?" asked Ethan.

"My problem? You're the problem. You're not following the rules."

"What rule have I broken?"

"I told you to keep your dick in your pants."

"My dick is still in my pants. Behind my zipper." Ethan held out his arms. "I've barely even touched her because every time I try, you push me away."

"You've done more than touch her. You were latched onto her tit like a starving newborn."

"I knew you weren't ready for this." Ethan shook his head.

"What the fuck do you mean by that? You're the one overstepping."

"I've done nothing outside of what we agreed to, and you know it." Ethan smiled but it wasn't friendly. "I should've known better. A threesome is fine and fun until you fall in love. Then it's hell."

"I'm not in love." But the jealousy raging inside him argued that point.

"Lie to yourself all you want but I'm done." Ethan walked past him toward the bedroom.

"You are not going in there without me." Harker followed.

Ethan gave him a disgusted look and then opened the door. Alison was sitting with the covers clutched to her breasts. Her eyes were wide and filled with uncertainty.

"Alison, I'm going to call it a night." Ethan smiled softly at her. "It was lovely. You were perfect. I'd love to say we can try again sometime but I don't think his"—he glanced at Harker—"jealousy is going to go away."

"I'm not jealous." Harker was going to punch Ethan.

Ethan sighed, shaking his head as he walked to the bed. "Then you won't mind if I do this." He bent, kissing Alison softly as he took her hands in his and raised them above her head. The covers slid to her waist, exposing her perfect breasts. Ethan began kissing his way down her throat.

Harker shouldn't care. This should be making him hard as a rock but instead he wanted to launch himself across the room and beat the lips off the other man.

Ethan let go of Alison's arms, his mouth trailing across the tops of her breasts as his hand slid under the covers toward her pussy. Her hand dropped to Ethan's head, her long fingers running through his hair. Harker knew exactly how fucking fabulous that felt and his jealousy exploded.

"That's enough." The sound of his voice was almost feral.

Ethan stopped immediately and straightened, giving Harker a condescending smirk. "Is that jealousy I hear in your growl?" He turned back to Alison. "Good night. I would say go easy on him. Feeling jealous isn't something men like us are used to, but since he fucking pissed me off,

I'd prefer you make his life a living hell." He walked across the room, stopping in the doorway. "Harker don't ever ask me to be the third to your party again."

Harker didn't move. He had no idea what to do with all these emotions. He wasn't good with emotions. Feelings were detrimental in business and in life. He'd thought he'd eliminated them but here they were raging through him again like when he'd been a kid—anger, fear, hurt, betrayal.

The sound of the door to the suite slamming shut reverberated through the room. Ethan was more than pissed and he couldn't blame him. He'd invited the other man to play. Everything had been fair game except vaginal and anal sex. One because they were trying to conceive, and the other had been a hard no from Alison.

Alison pulled up the sheet, covering her breasts. Her eyes were wide and filled with confusion but all he could see was the memory of her hand clutching Ethan's head, holding him as he sucked her breast.

"I suppose you want me to run after him and beg him to come back."

"Are you mad at me?" Her voice cracked. "Did I do something wrong?"

"Did you do something wrong? You heard Ethan. You were perfect." The anger raced out of his mouth like a dam bursting. "Clinging to him. Holding him close as you squirmed and moaned. From me." He slapped his chest. "Because I was eating your pussy. Not Ethan."

"Harker, why are you—"

"Why am I what? Upset? We agreed. No sex."

"We didn't…He didn't…"

"You sure as fuck wanted him too. Moaning and writhing, wanting his cock inside you."

"I never—"

"Don't fucking lie to me. You practically melted when the man touched you and when he took off his shirt? Fuck, I thought you were going to come."

She bit her lip and her eyes filled with tears.

He looked away and started to pace so he didn't have to see her cry because he was still too angry to stop. "Did you want to suck his dick? You do like doing that and you're fucking great at it. You're the best I've ever had but Ethan's had more. Maybe I should call him back to get his opinion."

Alison crawled out of bed, tucking the sheet around her.

"Where the fuck do you think you're going?" He wasn't done raging at her.

"I didn't do anything wrong. I don't deserve to be treated like this." She brushed past him.

"You are not leaving this room." Harker followed her.

"I am leaving this room." She dropped the sheet and grabbed her dress from the floor. "And you can't stop me."

"Really?" He strode over to her, letting her feel how much bigger and stronger he was than her. "I think I can."

She glared up at him as she stepped into her dress. "Debug. I'm done with this game and I'm done with you."

He almost snarled. He'd never wanted to ignore a

safeword as much as he did now, but he didn't move as she pushed past him and walked to the door.

"I guess your mom isn't as important as fucking Ethan. I should've figured that. You women do fall all over yourselves for him. Let me tell you a secret; he's not that fucking special. His dick is just like the rest of ours."

"Go to hell, Harker." She slammed the door as she left.

He started after her but stopped himself. He thumped his head against the door. What the fuck was wrong with him? He was a jackass. He needed to calm down, find her and apologize but if he saw her crying on Ethan's shoulder, he'd probably be a raving ass again.

CHAPTER 50: ALISON

Alison hurried down the hallway. She needed to get as far away from Harker as she could. She was so mad and hurt that she wanted to scream and cry at the same time, but she refused to do either of those until she got home. Then she'd probably do both. She reached for her keys.

Shit. She stopped. She didn't have her purse. It was in the room and so was her phone. She glanced over her shoulder, half expecting to see Harker barreling toward her, but the hallway was empty. She swallowed back her tears. She was glad he wasn't coming after her. She didn't want to speak to him ever again, but it still hurt that he didn't care even a little that he'd hurt her. Well, she certainly wasn't going back to the room. One of the bouncers at the door would call a cab for her.

She walked into the main room of the Club and headed for the doors but there was some kind of commotion at the entrance. The bouncers were both standing and talking to someone and they didn't look happy. Katie, the waitress, walked past her. "Excuse me."

"Hi," said Katie. "Would you like a drink?"

"Ah, no. Can I borrow your phone? I know. Who doesn't have a cell phone? I do but I left it in the room and...uhm, I'm not going back there."

"Oh." Katie seemed to understand. "I get it. I do but I don't have my phone. I left it at home with my sister. Check with Bea. There's one behind the bar that you can use."

"Okay. Thanks." She made her way through the crowded room, side-stepping and squirming her way up to the bar.

"Be right with you," said Bea as she passed by carrying several drinks.

Alison waited, every second seeming like an hour. The bartender whizzed by again and started making more drinks. Someone walked up behind her and she knew before he even spoke that it was Harker. It was like the air itself changed when he was near. Instead of being normal, breathable air it was charged with tension and excitement.

"Alison, I'm sorry. Please come back to the room with me so we can talk."

The man was unbelievable. She was never talking to him again after what he'd said to her. She spun around and he was so close that she brushed against him. "I'm not going anywhere with you. Ever again." His cologne surrounded her like when they were in bed, making her remember his face between her legs, his mouth doing the most delicious things to her body. She turned back toward the bar and inhaled deeply to clear her head.

"Please. I'm an idiot. A jackass." He moved closer, his

strong body pressing gently against her back.

She shifted forward away from him. Pissed off and horny was an explosive combination. She wasn't sure if she wanted to hit him or jump him.

"I owe you a better apology." His breath tickled her ear. "Please. Come back to the room with me. Just to talk."

"Go away."

"This is hard for me to admit." He rested his face against the side of her head. "I was jealous. I've never been jealous. Not like this."

"Not even with Merri," she whispered, her anger slipping a notch.

"No." His voice was rich and dark in her ear. "I was angry when she chose Tobias because I'd lost. I don't like to lose but this...this was different."

She swallowed the lump in her throat. "What you said...I didn't deserve that."

"I know." Again that soft touch of his cheek against her head. "I'm sorry. This was all my fault."

"You wanted to do this." She turned toward him. "How did you want me to act? Did you want me to not enjoy it?"

"No." He lifted his hand as if to touch her face but let it fall. "I wanted you to experience this. I want you to experience a lot of things. Pleasures you've never even imagined but...I didn't expect to feel...so angry." The person next to them moved away and he pushed to her side. "I've had threesomes before with...with women I've cared about and it was fine, but with you...I was furious when

Ethan touched you anywhere. Even your hand."

"Why?" Her heart did little flip-flops. She should be furious with him. She never allowed anyone to talk to her like he had but the sincerity and confusion in his face made her anger fade. She touched his cheek. "Why did it bother you."

"I don't know." He leaned into her hand. "It was bad enough the way you looked at him when he took off his shirt but when I saw you holding him to your breast"—he took her hand and kissed the tips of her fingers—"I lost it. You should've been holding me. Touching me. Not him."

"I want to be with you not Ethan."

"Really? Even though I'm Gus Barker? Your grumpy, old boss."

"Yes." Alison's anger fled completely at the uncertainty in his eyes.

"Let's go back to the room." The vulnerability in his gaze heated to something hot and dark as he turned.

"Oh, no." She pulled from his grasp. "You can't say those things and have me fall right back into your bed." She touched his cheek. "I mean this Harker. If you ever do anything like that again, this is over."

"I understand." He put his hand over hers. "And I won't. I didn't even mean it when I said it. I was angry and"—he swallowed, his vulnerability flashing in his dark eyes again—"hurt because I thought you wanted him and not me."

"Not an excuse."

"I know." He kissed her palm. "Let me make it up to

you." His lips touched her softly—hesitant, questioning.

She opened for him and his uncertainty exploded into desperate desire. He grasped her head, his tongue claiming her mouth as his. He pulled her against his hard chest. Her hands skimmed up his torso and then she pushed away, breaking the kiss.

"Let's get a table and have a drink." If she let this go any further, they'd be back in the suite and in bed.

"I'll pour you anything you want in the room."

"Not so fast. You have to earn the privilege of me going anywhere with you."

"What do you want? Name it and it's yours."

"I want to spend the night hearing all about the Club. All the secrets and scandals in explicit detail."

"Now, I really am in hell," muttered Harker.

CHAPTER 51: HARKER

"Oh, it won't be that bad and if it is, you deserve it."
Alison took Harker's hand. "Let's go get a table." She
hesitated. "Actually, let's stay at the bar."

"Okay." He pulled out a chair. "But why the change of
mind?" He'd been looking forward to tucking her away in a
dark corner and fucking her.

"It's safer here." She sat on the chair.

"Oh Alison, I thought you knew me better than that."
He sat next to her. "Nothing will keep me from getting
what I want." He leaned by her ear. "And I want you." He
turned back toward the bar and stopped one of the
bartenders as he walked by. "I'll have a double bourbon on
the rocks and Alison will have…" He turned toward her.

"Water."

"Water?" He frowned. A few drinks might help her
forget what an ass he'd been.

"Yeah." She smiled at the bartender. "Just water."

"Got it." The guy walked away to make their drinks.

She turned toward Harker. "I don't see any reason to
make this easier on you."

His gaze held hers. "I am sorry. I had absolutely no reason to say what I did."

"Don't do it again." She nodded, her eyes getting watery.

"I won't."

The bartender brought them their drinks and walked away. Harker took a sip and leaned closer to Alison. He needed to get her hot and horny and there was no better place to do that than here. "See that couple over there." He glanced across the bar.

"Where?" She looked around. "Which couple? There are a lot of couples here."

"Across the bar about four or five people to your right."

"Yeah." She leaned forward, watching them.

"They're about to have sex."

"What?" Her eyes almost popped from her skull. "No. How can you tell?" She took a sip of her water. "It just looks like he's standing behind her. He's close but not *that* close."

"See how his face is intense and he's focused on her and nothing else." He put his hand on her thigh, where the hem of her dress met her skin. "A fight could start right behind him and he'd ignore it." He ran his fingers across her smooth, warm skin, barely venturing beneath her dress. "See how she's leaning against the bar and he's moving closer. Watch her face. Tell me when he puts his dick inside her."

"Here? Really?" Alison's breathing increased as she

watched the couple.

"Absolutely." He drew circles on her leg, letting his fingernail scrape gently across her skin every now and then.

She inhaled sharply, her lips parting in a gasp as if the man had penetrated her.

"He's fucking her now, isn't he?" He let his fingers dip between her thighs and his cock hardened as her legs drifted apart for him.

"Yes," she whispered.

He tore his gaze away from her and looked at the couple. The man was going slow, the woman barely swaying from his thrusts. He leaned closer to Alison's ear. "There are others too. Look around the bar and tell me who's playing right now?" He kissed her neck. His hand moving slowly upward.

Alison's gaze moved across the bar. "That lady over there. The one with the red hair. Her face looks…uhm, like she's going to come but…" She turned toward him. She was so close that her breath teased across his lips. "I don't see a guy around. It could be another woman but…" She faced the woman again. "No one around her seems to be…participating." She turned back to him. "Is she masturbating?" Her face flushed a pretty pink, but her brown eyes were filled with curiosity. "Why would someone do that in public?"

"Some are exhibitionists but that's not what's going on with her."

"Then what is?" She looked back at the woman. "No one is paying any attention to her."

"Her partner doesn't have to be close."

"He doesn't?" Her head snapped toward him, her mouth so tempting and so close. "How is that possible?"

"Toys, Alison. He can control her orgasm from across the bar. Look around and find her partner."

She did, her luscious lips turning down in a frown. "I can't find him. What should I look for?"

"Oh honey, you have so much to learn. So much I can teach you."

"I suppose."

"I'll give you a hint." He kept his tone neutral, but he wanted to shout in triumph. She was going to forgive him.

"You will?"

"Yes, but it'll cost you."

"I think you owe me." She frowned but her eyes smiled. They were back to playing and that was excellent.

"I do, but I'll pay that debt later. Right now, I'd rather charge you."

"How much?"

"I don't want money."

"I know that." She laughed.

"So what you actually want to know is what I want."

"Now is not the time to be correcting my English, Harker, or should I call you Barker?"

"You should not." He touched her lips. "What I want is a kiss."

"Just a kiss." Her eyes dropped to his mouth and her tongue slipped out to wet her bottom lip.

He almost groaned as his cock hardened to the point of

pain. "Yes. A kiss."

"Maybe I'll find the guy on my own." She glanced around the bar. She was playing with him and he loved it—the anticipation, the uncertainty. She looked back at him. "I suppose one kiss won't hurt."

"Perfect. So you agree to a kiss?"

"Yes, I just said..." She paused, sensing the trap, but it was too late. She'd already agreed.

"You're right. You did." He squeezed her thigh as he skimmed the fingers of his other hand down her throat. She leaned toward him, her lips parting and her eyelids lowering. He tapped her nose. "I never said the kiss would be on your lips."

"What?" Her eyes snapped open.

"You heard me." He ran his hand from her neck down to her chest, tracing his fingers across her hardening nipple.

"Harker, we can't." She pushed his hand away. "Not here."

"We can. We will." He bent his head as he slowly pulled down her dress.

She grabbed the material, stopping him from baring her breast.

He glanced up at her. "I have no problem kissing you through your dress. Of course, it's going to get wet and then it'll be noticeable all night. But if I kiss your skin, once I'm done no one will know." He kissed the top of her breast, his tongue slipping under the neckline. "Your choice."

"We can't. I'm not ready for this." Her face was

scarlet.

"You're making a bigger deal of this than it is." He straightened. "But it's fine. I'll choose somewhere else to kiss." He skimmed his hand between her legs, almost to her pussy.

"Harker, stop." She grabbed his wrist.

"You have to get over this shyness." He moved his hand back to her knee. "Is it okay if I kiss your neck?"

"Yeah." She relaxed a bit, but she shouldn't because he knew exactly where to kiss her neck that'd make her forget everything but him.

"Good." He lowered his face, letting his breath tickle her skin.

She tipped her head a little and he kissed her neck. It wasn't a soft kiss. It was hot and wet. He licked her skin before sucking and biting gently. She moaned, making his dick push against his zipper. His hand slid back up her legs, stroking the warm flesh of her thighs. He nipped her neck and her legs opened for him. He sucked and nibbled, torturing that spot that made her wild as his hand crept closer and closer to her pussy.

"Harker. Stop."

Her legs closed, but he didn't remove his hand. He'd worked too hard to get here. He wasn't leaving that easily.

"It's okay. No one cares," he whispered in her ear, running his fingers back and forth on the petal soft skin of her inner thigh. "Look around. No one is even watching." He prayed that was the case. Most wouldn't pay much attention, but some would watch.

She gazed around the bar, her body softening, and his fingers finally made their way to her pussy. He stilled, grinning against her neck.

"You naughty girl. You didn't put on your panties."

"I was in a hurry." Her words were breathless as he stroked her with one long finger. "I was on my way home." She moaned softly as his thumb pressed down on her clit, rubbing the little nub that was already engorged for him.

He grabbed her chin and turned her face to his. His mouth captured hers, kissing her like she was his life, his air. His hand moved faster between her legs, and she relaxed, surrendering to him as she writhed under his caress.

CHAPTER 52: ALISON

Harker's kiss pulled Alison into a tidal wave of passion and his hands…Those talented fingers made the desire from earlier rage to life once again—stronger, hotter and more desperate for the release that'd been stolen from her.

His thumb teased her clit as he slid two fingers inside her, spreading them wide and stretching her. Her hips rocked against him, searching for release. Her fingers clasped his arm as he thrust into her body. His other hand grabbed her breast, pinching her hard nipple and she broke apart. Her orgasm washed through her as his fingers continued to pump slowly into her, and his kisses softened to whispers, trailing across her lips and cheeks.

She felt boneless and had no idea how she was even staying upright in the chair. Oh mercy. The chair. They were at the Club. At the bar. "I can't believe…Take me back to the room."

"Gladly." He took her hand and tugged.

She didn't move. "Take my arm."

"Why?" He sighed. "Alison, open your eyes."

"Nope. Never." She squeezed them tighter together.

"No one is looking." He kissed her eyelids. "No one cares. I swear. Please, trust me."

"Do I have to?"

"Yes." He chuckled.

"Fine." She opened her eyes. A couple of people glanced at her, but Harker hadn't lied. No one was looking at them. "I can't believe no one noticed."

"They noticed but it's not a big deal. The stage is the show. The rest…is just pleasure." He tugged on her hand again. "Come. Let's go back to the room."

She didn't move. This was…exciting…dangerous but not really because no one cared what they did. Her eyes skimmed down his frame. He was as aroused as she'd been. She pulled her hand from his hand before running her fingers down his abdomen and across his erection. He was long and hard and more than ready.

"Alison." The word was a warning.

"I changed my mind. I don't want to go back to the room yet." She gave him a little squeeze, loving how his eyes darkened. "I'm not completely ready to forgive you.

"I'm past playing."

"Too bad because I'm not." She smiled up at him, her fingers skimming below the waistband of his pants.

"Don't start something you aren't going to finish."

"I could say that exact same thing to you. I'm sure Ethan would agree with me."

"I explained why I did what I did."

"Yes, and I accepted the explanation, but it doesn't mean I'm happy about it."

"Me either. I don't like being jealous."

"Funny, because I like that you were jealous." She'd been so sure that he couldn't truly care for her, if he were willing to share her with another man. This made her fill with hope that he did…perhaps…feel something more than desire for her.

"Don't get used to it. I'm sure I'll get over it."

"Oh. Right." The little fluttering of hope in her chest was squashed like a bug on the windshield. She moved her hand away, but he captured her wrist.

"Alison, I'm sorry." He kissed her fingers. "This is new for me…these feelings. I hate feelings."

"We all do." She was scared too.

"But you're used to having emotions. I'm not. I quit feeling anything but competitive a long time ago."

"I know it's scary but it's good too. Right?" She needed to know that he wanted this with her.

"I guess, but how about we start with a feeling I'm used to." He put her hand back on his cock.

"You're so…incorrigible." She couldn't help but squeeze him as she ran her hand up and down his length.

"Unbutton my pants. If you have the guts."

"If I have guts?" She knew he was baiting her with the challenge, but she was happy to best him.

"Yeah." He shrugged. "I don't think you do. I think you're teasing me."

"And if that's what I'm doing, it's fine because you owe me."

"I do and I'll put up with your teasing as long as I

can."

"Oh, really? And then what will you do?" She was getting wet just thinking about pushing him past his control.

"Not sure. It could be a couple of things. I might pick you up, toss you over my shoulder and head to the room. Or I might pull you off that chair, push you against the bar and fuck you right here."

"Since when did you become such a barbarian?" Her insides tingled at the thought. She should be appalled but her body wanted him to claim her in every conceivable way.

He leaned down by her ear. "It's barbaric but it's making you hot. Isn't it?"

"I neither confirm nor deny that statement." She grinned at him as she unbuttoned his pants.

She glanced around. Except for the people directly across from them she was shielded by Harker's large body. She could do this. She wanted to do this. She unzipped his pants and pulled out his cock, loving his heat and the smoothness as she stroked him. Her eyes lifted to his as she slowly licked her lips. His dark gaze dropped to her mouth. His chest heaved as he waited. She lowered her head. His hand touched her hair, pushing her downward.

"Harker? Is that you?" asked a woman.

Alison sat up like a jack-in-the-box.

A tall, thin, beautiful woman with dark hair pushed up to the bar by them. Her eyes widened as they landed on Alison. "Oh my god. I'm so sorry. I swear, I didn't see you.

If I had, I never would've…" Her eyes sparkled like she was going to burst out laughing any minute. "I'm sorry. Really. I'm going to back away and pretend this never happened."

"No. Don't." Alison had no idea why those words came out of her mouth. Having this woman leave would be the least embarrassing thing for all of them, but the words were out there now and there was no going back. "I'm Alison." She held out her hand. "And you are?"

CHAPTER 53: HARKER

"Going." Harker needed Dahlia to leave now. "She's leaving."

"Yes, he's right. I should go." Dahlia wasn't a stupid woman.

"No. Please. Stay. Harker never introduces me to anyone," said Alison.

"Ah…I think you two have better things to do." Dahlia glanced downward.

Alison followed her gaze. "Harker, put that away." She waved her hand at his crotch where his dick still stuck out of his pants, not as hard as before but still raring to go.

"What? Dahlia's right. We have better things to do."

"Stop being rude." Alison gave him an exasperated look and then turned toward Dahlia. "Please, don't worry about interrupting. Believe me, the moment is over."

"Not for me," he grumbled as he forced his very unhappy cock back into his pants and zipped up.

Alison ignored him. "I just started coming here a few weeks ago and Harker hasn't introduced me to anyone. Not really. I did meet Bea and"—she gave him a mischievous glance—"Ethan but I want to meet other people."

"You don't need to know anyone but me." Especially, his ex-lovers.

"Relax." Alison touched his arm, her eyes darting between the two. "I'm assuming by the uneasy looks that the two of you had a relationship. It's okay. I don't mind. I knew you weren't a virgin when we met."

Dahlia choked on a laugh.

"Neither were you, but I don't expect to become friends with your ex-lovers." He'd probably strangle them if he ever had the misfortune of meeting any of them.

"That's because you're a jealous jerk." Alison's brow raised in challenge and Harker bit his tongue. "But I'm not. So stop being rude and introduce me to your friend. You owe me."

"Alison this is Dahlia. Dahlia this is Alison." He really, really was starting to dislike intelligence in women. Alison had found the perfect hell to punish him for his earlier jealousy.

"Nice to meet you." Dahlia held out her hand, her eyes dropping to Alison's ring.

"Nice to meet you too," said Alison. "I take it you and Harker were—"

"Dom and sub," said Dahlia.

"Oh. I was going to say dating." Alison's face heated.

"Sorry." Dahlia winced. "I obviously spend way too much time here. I'm not used to talking like a normal person."

"Don't apologize. I knew you didn't just date and your

explanation is so much more descriptive."

Harker wanted to crawl under the bar and hide. He knew women well enough to know that although this seemed fine, it wasn't.

Dahlia smiled. "I suppose you could call it dating even though"—she glanced at him—"we never actually went anywhere."

"Really? How long were you two together?" asked Alison.

"A little over a year," said Dahlia.

"A year and you never went on a date." Alison turned toward Harker. "Not once? What's wrong with you?"

"It wasn't that kind of relationship." He shouldn't have to explain his prior sexual commitments to his wife.

"Harker, stop being an ass." Alison glared at him.

"No. He's right." Dahlia's eyes were filled with hurt. "Ours was just a sexual relationship."

"Dahlia, don't." Harker wanted to strangle both women. "It was more than that and you know it."

Alison stiffened and Harker had to fight not to flee. He was in a no-win situation.

"No, Harker. You made it perfectly clear what our relationship was. If I thought that there could've been more maybe I would've stuck around." Dahlia turned toward Alison. "It was nice meeting you, but I should go."

"I'm sorry. I shouldn't have brought up the past," said Alison.

"It's okay," said Dahlia. "The past is the past."

"It is and we should leave it there." Alison smiled.

"Are you here with someone? Friends? A new boyfri...dom?"

"No, not tonight." Dahlia smiled but it was sad.

"No one is alone at the Club unless he or she wants to be." Harker was ready for this group chat to be done.

Alison frowned at him and shifted, excluding him from the conversation. "Please stay and have a drink with us. I promise not to bring up the past or your relationship." She stood. "We'll get a table."

"Now, you want to get a table?" Harker gave her a disgusted look. Before they could've fucked at the table, but Alison wasn't ready to do that in front of his former sub.

"Ignore him." Alison took Dahlia's arm and headed for a table. "Although I'm sure I don't have to tell you how grumpy the man can be when he doesn't get his way."

"I thought we were leaving the past in the past." Harker grabbed their drinks and followed after them.

"You're grumpy now," said Alison. "So it's not the past."

"I don't recall him ever not getting his way." Dahlia gave her an odd look.

"Oh. Yeah, I guess that would've been frowned upon in the relationship you had. You know dom/sub and all that."

"It's frowned upon in our relationship too," he muttered. "Not that it makes a damn bit of difference."

Alison glanced at Dahlia and they both laughed, making Harker's hell complete.

CHAPTER 54: HARKER

Harker sat at his personal table in hell while his former sub, Dahlia, chatted with his wife, Alison. Normally, it wouldn't bother him when an old girlfriend met a new one. He'd had subs compare notes plenty of times. Sometimes it'd even turned into a threesome, but that wouldn't happen this time. After tonight's fiasco, he was done with threesomes.

"Harker. Dahlia." Richard, another member of the Club, walked up to their group. "How nice to see you tonight." His eyes went to Alison.

Harker sighed. He'd just descended to the next level in hell. Richard was an older man who he usually enjoyed talking to, but the guy was a nosy bastard who could root out gossip like a pig found truffles. "Alison this is Richard. Richard this is my wife, Alison."

"Nice to meet you." Alison stood and shook Richard's hand.

"I'd heard you got married." Richard clasped both of Alison's hands in his "But I hadn't quite believed it. However, now I understand." His eyes darted to Dahlia.

215

"The heart can be a tricky thing because your previous sub was quite marry-worthy too."

"Thank you, Richard," said Dahlia. "But I don't need my ego boosted nor my feelings coddled. Alison and I are friends."

Harker rolled his eyes. Just what he needed. His former sub as his wife's best friend. That spelled disaster for him.

"I wouldn't have expected anything else from you Dahlia." Richard smiled kindly. "And Alison, since I don't know you, I wouldn't have expected anything but I'm glad everyone is acting like adults."

"It'd be stupid to act any other way," said Alison. "It's not like I didn't have lovers before Harker, and I knew at his age he certainly wasn't a virgin." Her face flushed. "Not that he's old or anything."

Harker pictured himself pulling out a chair at his hell-table for his wife as she tried to yammer her way out of this crater sized hole she'd created. Richard was considerably older than he was.

"Not that age has much to do with that. I mean, unless you're like ten or something. Obviously, none of us are that young. Or virgins." Alison continued to ramble as Richard's gaze slid to Harker.

"She talks a lot." He shrugged.

Alison's mouth snapped shut so fast he heard her teeth clank.

Pissing her off might be the best way to get out of this conversation. "Especially when she's nervous." He shook his head. "I swear sometimes she never shuts up."

Richard's eyes narrowed, his gaze confused and slightly appalled as he turned back toward Alison. "I find it refreshing when a woman speaks her mind."

"Thank you." Alison sent Harker a dirty look. "Would you like to join us?"

Harker considered getting a ball gag for his wife, but it wasn't her fault. She didn't know that Richard spent his free time poking his nose into everyone's business. The man knew everything about everyone, and he had to be curious about Harker's sudden marriage. Richard would pepper them with innocuous questions that'd end up stinging like a swarm of hornets.

"Thank you. I did want to talk to Harker about that contract." Richard sat on the chair next to him. "My lawyer will be sending it back to yours. There are some major modifications that need to be agreed upon before I sign."

"Major modifications? About what? We agreed on everything that's in the contract."

"Everything except those loopholes you added." Richard shook his head. "I have no idea why I do business with you."

Harker snorted. "Because I make you a ton of money."

"No, that's not it." Richard tapped his fingers on the chair. "I already have a ton of money."

"One can never have enough money," he said.

"True, but I think I continue to do business with you because I love the perverse challenge of finding all those perfectly worded clauses and addendums." Richard laughed. "Your contracts are notorious for allowing you to

217

wriggle out of everything and I love finding every single one and making you remove it."

"I don't wriggle out of anything."

"Unless the deal goes south. Then I've seen you wriggle like a worm fleeing a bird."

"I protect my assets. It's good business." He never used the addendums unless he had to.

"That's true and I do commend you for that." Richard turned toward Alison. "I hope you were careful when you signed that prenup."

"We didn't have a prenup." She took a drink of her water.

"No prenup?" Richard's head almost snapped off his neck as he swung toward Harker.

"Oh. No. I mean that we would've except…" Alison's face flushed. "We…ah…we signed a contract instead. It's like a prenup. I guess. So, yeah. I was careful."

Richard gave him a confused look before turning back toward Alison. "Then I hope you had a lawyer look it over carefully."

"Our contract was pretty straight forward." Alison's face paled.

"With Harker's money nothing is simple or straight forward," said Richard.

"Our contract is fine." He didn't need Alison reading the damn thing again. "I wouldn't use a loophole on my wife." He may have put them in, but he wouldn't use them.

"Of course not," said Richard.

It was clear that the other man didn't believe that at all

and now Alison was getting suspicious. He should've never brought her here. No, he should've never let her leave their room. She wouldn't have if he hadn't gotten jealous. He never got jealous. What was happening to him? He wasn't an emotional man, but this woman was exploding through his life and ripping him apart from the inside out.

"Enough about contracts," said Dahlia.

"You're right," said Richard. "Business is boring." He smiled and Harker braced for the next blow because Richard's eyes only gleamed like that when he was going in for the kill. "Let's talk about your marriage. So where did the two of you go on your honeymoon?"

"We stayed here." Harker was going to hear it now and he was in no mood for a lecture.

"You didn't take your bride anywhere?" Richard shook his head. "Let me give you some advice—"

CHAPTER 55: ALISON

"I don't need your advice." Harker's soft voice sent alarm bells ringing through Alison.

"We were going to." She jumped in because if Richard kept annoying Harker, their night would be over soon. "But I had too much work. Mac, who Harker hired"—she sent him a soft smile—"has been a big help but we're still behind."

"You work for Harker and you still married him?" Richard didn't even try to hide his surprise.

"Yes, she's the head of our software engineering department," said Harker.

She frowned at him but correcting him would bring up questions she really didn't want to answer.

"Smart and beautiful. A most potent combination," said Richard.

"Very." Harker's dark eyes filled with the promise of pleasure that almost made Alison jump up, grab his hand and drag him back to their room.

"The problem you have Harker—"

"I don't have a problem," said Harker.

Richard continued as if he hadn't spoken. "Is that smart women don't stay with stupid men who don't appreciate them."

"Alison knows how much I appreciate her." His eyes moved back to her and she wanted to agree but she wasn't sure she did know that.

"I don't know how she would when you didn't take her on a honeymoon. That's the absolute least a husband can do for his bride."

"Alison understands and you should mind your own business," said Harker.

"Yes, I should but where's the fun in that." Richard grinned.

"No. Really. It's okay." Alison laughed. "We are super busy at work and our marriage was kind of hurried."

"Really?" Richard's eyes immediately dipped to Alison's stomach.

"There's no reason to explain our relationship to anyone." Harker's words were clipped.

"Oh. Okay. Sorry but I figured they knew since they already knew you got…" She turned to Richard. "How did you hear about our wedding?"

"Harker was a confirmed bachelor. Trust me, this story is making its way around the Club," said Richard.

"Dahlia? Did you know too? You didn't seem surprised when you saw the ring on my finger?"

"Yes. Ethan told me." Dahlia's eyes darted to Harker so fast that Alison almost missed it.

"Ethan?" She winced as she looked at Harker. It made

sense. Harker had to have told him earlier. Ethan had her membership contract ready the last time they were here, but the other man was still a bit of a sore subject between the two of them.

"It's not like it was a secret." Harker's tone made it clear he wasn't happy about this conversation.

"You're right and that's why I don't understand why you didn't want me to bring it up. You're the one who came here on our wedding night."

Richard's eyes widened as if he'd just heard the biggest, juiciest secret. Harker's reaction was quite different. It was like he'd turned to stone, but she really didn't care. Everyone had probably already heard about that and she'd rather it was clear that she knew. She hated looking like a fool.

"You came here on your wedding night," said Richard. "Please tell me the two of you came here together to…celebrate."

"My bride and I had a disagreement." The words were almost forced from Harker's mouth.

"Enough to leave her on your wedding night?" Richard shook his head, but his eyes were gleaming with amusement. "I've been married several times and I've had my share of disagreements but that must've been a doozy."

"It was." Harker glared at Alison. "But we've gotten past it and before you ask another hundred questions, that's all either of us is going to say on that topic."

If looks could kill, Alison was pretty sure she'd be lying on the couch in a lifeless heap.

"Of course." Richard raised his glass to his lips and mumbled, "I'm sure I can get the details from someone."

Alison couldn't help it, she laughed. She glanced at Dahlia who sat quietly, staring at her hands in her lap. Unlike Richard, Dahlia didn't seem surprised to hear Harker had been here on their wedding night. Her good humor fled. "Dahlia, you mentioned that you live in Europe."

Richard frowned at the change of topic, but Dahlia jumped on it like a lifeline.

"It's wonderful. You get to see new things and experience new customs. You can take weekend trips to other countries. I'd recommend living abroad to everyone, at least for a few years."

"Sounds lovely." She glanced at Harker who was watching her closely. "When did you come back to the states?" Harker's face tightened and Alison wanted to cry. Her instincts were never wrong.

"Oh...uhm." Dahlia stared straight at Alison as if she were afraid to look anywhere else. "I don't remember the exact day, but it was a couple of weeks ago."

"Are you planning on staying?" Richard seemed oblivious to the underlying tension.

"Ah...probably not. Things didn't work out how I'd hoped, so I'll be going back soon." This time Dahlia's eyes did dart to Harker for one quick second.

If Alison hadn't been watching, she would've missed it. In that moment she knew without doubt that Dahlia had come back for Harker. She wasn't sure how to feel about that. Her marriage wasn't real, but sometimes, the way he looked at her, made her think that they had a chance to make it real.

"Alison Robinson?" A man stopped by her side.

"Dan?" she stood. "Oh my god. I haven't seen you since college." She hugged him. "How's Lisa? Is she here?" She glanced around.

"We're not together anymore," said Dan.

"Really? Everyone thought the two of you would marry and have a hundred kids."

"Me too." He smiled but it was sad.

"Oh. I'm so sorry." She winced. "You know me. I never seem to be able to keep my mouth shut."

"Except when introducing your husband." Harker walked over to stand behind her, holding out one hand while placing the other possessively on the small of her back.

"Dan Ridgeway." Dan shook Harker's hand.

"Harker. Alison's husband."

"I got that part." Dan grinned.

"Just wanted to make sure." Harker squeezed Alison's waist.

"Stop it." She slapped his arm, but she loved this jealous side of him. "We married recently and…well, I guess, I can't take him anywhere."

"You'll take me everywhere." Harker's hand slid to her ass. "Especially here."

"I don't blame you on that. The Club is safe but"—Dan's eyes darted to Dahlia—"if I weren't single, I wouldn't let my girlfriend come here without me. Too many eligible men around. Doctors. Businessmen. Lawyers, like me."

"I'd heard you passed the bar exam. Congratulations." Alison had to fight to stop from laughing at how Dan was making it clear that he was single, eligible and interested in Dahlia.

"Thanks. I landed a great job too." He pulled out his wallet and handed her a card. "I work for the best divorce lawyer around. We do other things too but my boss—"

"Speaking of your boss," said Richard. "Is Terry here tonight? I need to talk to him."

"Hey Richard, nice to see you," said Dan. "But no. I don't think Terry's here. As far as I know he was planning a weekend with Maggie and her kids. Maybe next weekend when her ex has the kids."

Alison had nowhere to put Dan's business card, so she handed it to Harker. He started to toss it on the nearby table, and she slapped his arm.

"Put it in your pocket."

"You don't need a divorce lawyer." But he slid it into his back pants pocket.

"I might if you don't stop acting like a jerk." She smiled at him and then turned back to Dan. "It seems you know everyone except Dahlia." She may as well help Dan out. He was a nice guy and if the other woman focused on him, she'd get over Harker faster. "Dahlia this is Dan. We went to college together. He's a great guy. Smart. Hard working. Funny. Loyal."

"Jesus," said Harker. "You make him sound like a dog."

Richard laughed and Dan's face heated.

"Oh...no. I mean. He's..."

"It's nice to meet you." Dahlia leaned forward and shook his hand. "I think those qualities are excellent in a man."

"Dan, why don't you join us." Alison sat, patting the seat between her and Dahlia.

"Ah..." Dan's eyes darted around the group.

Richard shook his head slightly.

"Maybe later," said Dan. "I told a friend I'd meet..."

Richard cleared his throat.

"Is everything okay?" She glared at Richard. "Do you need a drink of water or something?" Why did he care if Dan wanted Dahlia?

"No, thank you. I'm fine." Richard's grayish-blue eyes twinkled.

"Hmm." She gave him a warning look as she stood again. "I'm going to use the ladies' room. Dahlia, would you like to join me?"

"Sure." Dahlia stood.

"And Dan, definitely stop back by later." She took Dahlia's arm and led her away. As soon as they were out of hearing distance she said, "Dan is a great guy. Seriously. In college he was the one guy we could count on. Always. He'd help us with homework. Come and get us from parties if we were too drunk. He is a really, really nice guy...but sexy too. He has a great smile and a good job."

"Enough already." Dahlia laughed. "I let him know I was interested. Now—"

"You did? When?" How had she missed that?

"When I told him that his dog-like qualities were sexy."

"Oh god. I did make him sound like a dog, didn't I?"

"Only a little." Dahlia smiled.

"So are you going to go find him?"

"No. Now, it's up to him."

"Why? Why is it always up to the man?"

"It isn't for everyone, but for me, it is. I'm a sub. I like to be pursued, wooed and eventually captured. Then I submit." Dahlia frowned slightly. "I'm not sure Dan is quite ready for the full-on dominant roll yet. He seems new to all this."

"Is that a problem? I'm new to it and it doesn't bother Harker."

Dahlia's eyes clouded with sadness.

"Damn it. I'm so sorry. I shouldn't have brought him up." She was a horrible person.

"No. Don't be sorry. I'm glad you and Harker found each other."

"Thank you. I know this can't be easy for you." Alison knew firsthand what it was like to be the one not chosen. It'd happened to her all her life.

"It isn't. I was in love with him. I left because he wasn't the marrying kind. I knew if I didn't go, I would've stayed with him until he tired of me. Part of me hoped that he'd miss me enough to come after me, but he didn't."

Dahlia took Alison's hand. "I'm glad he found you. I think you're good for him."

"Oh, I'm not sure he'd agree with that," she said, trying to lighten the mood. "We definitely have our challenges."

"I'm sure you do. You work with him, live with him and sleep with him. I think calling it challenging is an understatement."

"Some days I want to strangle him." Alison laughed as they stepped into the restroom.

On the way back to the table Dahlia smiled at Alison and said, "I'm so glad we met."

"Me too. I don't have a lot of female friends."

"Me either," said Dahlia. "Most women are so catty, and I have to admit that I didn't want to like you. When I first heard that Harker was married, I was furious and hurt. He'd always told me he'd never marry." She smiled sadly. "I guess, he just meant that he'd never marry me."

Maybe she should tell the other woman that their marriage wasn't real, but what if she were wrong? What if it could be real?

"I want you to know that no matter how angry and jealous I was I wouldn't have slept with him. I swear as soon as Ethan told me Harker had gotten married, I was out of there."

"Oh. I'm sure. When exactly was this?" Alison tried to

keep her face impassive as everything inside her shattered.

Dahlia's words died in her throat. "I said too much. I shouldn't have said anything." She started walking faster.

"Wait." Alison grabbed her arm. "I need to know when this was." Her mind scrambled, trying to think of a night that they hadn't been together. Even that first week, he'd stayed home. Had he snuck out in the middle of the night? "Please, I need to know if he's coming here without me."

"I shouldn't say anything else. I wouldn't have said anything at all, but you knew he'd been here on your wedding night. I assumed the two of you had talked about it."

"So this"—she waved her hand—"whatever it was happened on my wedding night?"

"Yes," said Dahlia.

"Has he been here since then?"

"I've only seen him here tonight and one other time with you."

"Do you come here a lot?"

"More than I should." Dahlia smiled sadly.

"Okay. Thank you." She started back for the table.

"Seriously, Alison." Dahlia followed her. "Nothing happened between Harker and me that night. Nothing."

"Because Ethan stopped it."

Dahlia opened her mouth and closed it. "I didn't know he was married."

"No, but he did." Part of her died right then because although nothing had happened, it hadn't been Harker's choice and he'd lied to her.

CHAPTER 56: HARKER

"You're in trouble," said Richard.

"What?" Harker followed the other man's gaze. "Oh fuck." He knew women and that look on Alison's face as she and Dahlia made their way through the crowd meant very bad things for him.

"Even at the Club having your new wife hang out with your former sub is not a good idea."

"No shit, Richard. I tried to stop it."

"You should've tried harder." Richard leaned back taking a sip of his drink. "Although, I have to say it's going to be fun to watch you squirm like a worm surrounded by hens."

"I'll remember you said that when we modify the contract."

Richard laughed and both men stood as the women approached and sat down on the couch.

"Welcome back. We were just discussing worms and birds." Richard glanced at Harker from the corner of his eye. "How do you ladies feel about worms?"

"Worms?" Dahlia's nose wrinkled. "They're fine if

they stay in the ground and away from me."

"Alison?" asked Richard.

"Ah…" She cleared her throat. "They're very beneficial to soil and nature. I save them whenever I find them on the sidewalk. I hate seeing them surrounded by ants." She made a face. "What a horrible way to die. Torn apart by hundreds of tiny little bites."

"You have a soft heart. That's one of the things I admire most about you." He had no idea what had gone on in the bathroom between the women, but it was time to try and make up some ground. However, instead of looking at him and giving him one of her smiles that made his heart swell along with his cock she turned to Richard.

"What about you? What do you think about worms?"

"I think they're fun to watch." Richard's eyes sparkled.

"Really? How? On TV or something? Do they have worm houses like ant houses where you can watch them through glass?"

"Yeah, Richard?" He may as well not be the only one uncomfortable. "How do you watch worms?"

"Like she said, but enough about worms," said Richard. "Let's talk about men."

"My favorite topic." Dahlia's tone was upbeat but when her eyes met Harker's she had that *I'm so sorry* look on her face that he knew too well.

"Have you noticed that Anthony is without a sub again?" asked Richard.

"Already?" Dahlia glanced in the direction that Richard was looking.

"We all knew that wouldn't last long," said Harker. "She was just a diversion until he found someone else."

"Excuse me." Alison stood, smiling at Richard and Dahlia. "It was a pleasure to meet both of you but I'm tired."

"Mrs. Harker"—Richard stood taking her hand and kissing her fingers—"it was a pleasure."

Harker stood, stepping toward her.

"No stay. Have fun." Her eyes were brittle as she held out her hand. "I just need the key to the room."

"Nonsense." There was no way he was letting her go and mull over whatever had happened. He needed to be with her to figure out how much trouble he was in.

"No. Please don't." Her voice cracked a little, but he wasn't sure if she was going to cry or scream at him. "Just give me the key."

"I'll escort you." He took her hand. "Richard. Dahlia. Good night."

Dahlia stood and hugged Alison and then Harker, whispering. "I'm sorry. I thought she knew."

That was the only hint he had before Alison pulled her hand from his and walked away.

CHAPTER 57: ALISON

Alison walked as fast as she could without running but it made no difference. With his long legs Harker had no trouble keeping up with her. Fortunately, he didn't say a word. He just trailed behind her. She stopped at the entrance to their suite. The place where everything had turned into a nightmare.

He opened the door and stepped aside, letting her precede him into the room. He closed the door behind him and stood there, still not saying a word. The ass was probably waiting for her to speak first but she'd happily die before talking to him ever again–no matter how much she liked to talk.

She looked around the room. She'd been so nervous when they'd arrived that she had no idea where she'd left her purse. Her gaze stopped near the couch. Her purse was on the floor, partially under the sofa as if kicked aside. She knew exactly how it felt—unwanted, tossed away like trash. She hurried across the room, snatched it from the floor and walked toward the door. No one else may want that purse, but she did and that was enough.

"Where do you think you're going?"

"I'm going home." She choked on a laugh. What was she talking about? She had no home. "Or to my room at your house." She grabbed the door handle. "But don't worry. You can stay here and play with your ex-sub. Oh, I'm sorry. That's right. She's not interested in you right now because she's a decent person who doesn't have sex with married men."

"Fuck." His jaw clenched.

"Yeah. Fuck. I know everything."

"It's not what you think."

"How stupid do you think I am?" She couldn't believe his gall.

"Alison, please. Sit down and let's talk about this."

"There's nothing to talk about." Only her anger kept her from falling apart. She was such a fool. She'd been so sure that he'd been starting to truly care about her but all he'd been doing since the beginning was lying to her.

"Nothing happened on our wedding night. Nothing. At all. Not with you and not with Dahlia or anyone else."

"Don't you dare bring this back to me."

"Why not? It was your fault that I was here."

"My fault?" She'd never wanted to hit someone as much as she did now. "You're an adult. You chose to come here and to look for someone to fuck on your wedding night."

"Yes, I did. I should've…would've rather been home fucking my wife but she didn't want me." He almost shouted. "She didn't even consider me a man."

"I'm not apologizing for that again. I wasn't the one who left you to be with my ex."

"I had no idea she was here."

"Oh, lucky you."

"Hardly."

"That's right. Ethan stopped your luck."

"You annihilated my luck. Ethan only stopped me from alleviating my blue balls."

"Go to hell."

"Why not? Apparently, I bought an express pass when I married you."

"Oh...oh...you..." She had no response to that. She wasn't the reason he was in hell. This was his fault. Not hers.

He opened the door and stepped into the hallway. "Are you coming or are you going to stand there all night pretending to be a fish?"

She clamped her mouth shut before saying, "I'm not going anywhere with you."

"Then I guess you don't want to go home. Maybe you want to go back into the Club and find your old high school boyfriend."

"College and he wasn't my boyfriend but maybe I should. At least Dan's faithful." She pushed past him.

"Do it and the contract is void." He followed her down the hallway.

"Ha. Did you even think of that when you went looking to cheat? Mr. Business almost broke the contract before twenty-four hours were up."

"I'd never break a contract."

"Never? Maybe you should re-read it because it started when we married, not when we consummated the wedding vows. You owe Ethan a great big thank you because if he hadn't stopped you, you would've broken this contract." She shot him a glare. "I'd be a very rich woman right now and wouldn't ever have to let you touch me again if Ethan knew how to mind his own business. I need to have a private word with him and—"

"That's not going to happen." He grabbed her arm, his grip almost painfully tight.

"You don't own me." She yanked on her arm, trying to get away from him. "I can talk to whomever—"

He grabbed her other arm and pulled her to his chest, lifting her off her toes. "You are my wife."

"Fake wife." She was furious but her traitorous body didn't care. All it knew was that this man could give it pleasure beyond anything she'd ever had. She tried to ignore the feel of his hard body as he let her slide back down to her feet.

"You're still my wife." He kept hold of one of her arms as he strode down the hallway.

"Your fake wife who'll talk to anyone she wants." She stumbled along, almost running to keep from being dragged behind him.

"Try it. I dare you." He stared down at her, his dark eyes furious.

"Oh believe me, I'll talk to whomever I want, whenever I want." She frowned. "As soon as you let me go."

"Perfect because that's never going to happen."

CHAPTER 58: HARKER

Harker followed Alison into the house. She hadn't said one word on the way home. He walked into the living room, preparing himself for the upcoming battle but Alison went straight to the bedroom. That was fine with him because he was tired of fighting with her over the same damn thing. He went into the library and poured himself a drink.

He turned as he heard her walk past. "What the hell are you doing?"

"Going to bed." She clutched her pillow to her chest.

"Your bed is in our room."

"No. That's your bed. My room and my bed are down the hallway." Her chin jutted out.

"Alison, don't push me on this." His hand tightened on his glass.

She shook her head and walked away.

He stepped into the hallway. "This is not over."

She held her middle finger up over her shoulder.

"Don't make promises you don't intend to keep." He shouted.

She opened the bedroom door and turned, glaring at him. "You should follow your own advice." She walked inside, slamming the door.

"Oh, trust me. I keep all my promises." He took a sip of his bourbon. "Including sleeping with my wife."

CHAPTER 59: ALISON

Alison woke slowly. She was warm and comfortable with Harker's arm tossed over her chest. Her eyes flew open. Harker's arm shouldn't be in here. He shouldn't be in here, but there he was. Sound asleep on his stomach, his large body stretched out on her bed in her room.

She picked up his arm and dropped it to the side as she sat up. He mumbled something in his sleep as he slid his hand under the pillow. The blankets were around his waist and his back was bare—all that smooth, warm skin begging for her to run her fingers across it.

No. She got out of bed. She wasn't touching him unless it was to kill him for crawling into her bed when he knew she didn't want him near her. She tripped over his pants as she headed for the door. The man was a slob. She grabbed them and something fell out of his pocket as she threw them at his head. The big jerk didn't even flinch. She bent and picked up the paper from the floor. It was Dan's business card.

She started to toss it on the dresser but stopped. Harker would throw it away and Dan was her friend. She'd love to catch up with him and she didn't care if Harker liked it or not. She could talk to anyone she wanted. Maybe she'd see if Dan wanted to meet for brunch or something.

Alison stared at her computer, unable to focus. After she'd gotten up she'd showered, grabbed some toast and had gone to her office to work. Unfortunately, she wasn't getting anything done. Nothing about last night made any sense. When she'd first heard he'd gone to the sex club she'd never truly believed that he'd gone there to have sex with someone. Not because she'd thought he'd be loyal to her. Their marriage was fake after all, but because it'd break the contract. Harker would never break a contract. The fact that the only reason he hadn't was because Ethan had stopped him went against everything she knew about him.

She picked up Dan's card from her desk. She wasn't sure she wanted to do this, but she absolutely hated not knowing the answer to anything. She texted Dan.

ALISON: Hey, do you have a minute to talk?

She put her phone down. He was probably still sleeping. Maybe he and Dahlia had hooked up. Her phone beeped.

DAN: Who is this?
ALISON: Sorry. It's Alison.

Her phone rang and her hand trembled as she answered it.

"Hey Alison, what's up?" Dan asked.

"You sound awful chipper for a man who was at the bar last night."

"I don't drink much, and I don't need a lot of sleep."

"That's right. You never slept much in college. Did you?"

"Nope. Works great with this career."

"I bet." She laughed.

"So what's up. I don't think you called me this early to talk about my sleep habits."

"No. I'm sorry. I hate to ask this. I know we haven't talked in a long time and if you don't want to do it, just tell me. I'll understand."

"Alison, is everything okay?"

She almost cried at the concern in his voice. He was such a nice guy. "I don't know. You know I'm married and before we married, we signed a contract."

"A prenup. It's common especially for people with Harker's kind of money. You did have a lawyer, right?"

"No."

"Oh, Alison."

"I know. I know. Harker told me to hire one, but I didn't think I needed to. I trusted him and..."

"And now things aren't so great. I get that."

"Is that what happened with you and Lisa?"

"Yeah. Kind of. Things fizzled out. I guess, I wasn't

the one for her. She wanted someone more…exciting."

"She's a fool."

"No. They were right at the Club. When someone describes me, they can use those same terms to describe a dog."

"That's not true." She felt horrible. Harker was such an ass for saying it.

"Yes, it is." There was a smile in his tone.

"People love dogs."

"True." He laughed.

"And women grow up and exciting isn't as attractive as someone you can trust." Her voice cracked. She'd thought she could trust Harker.

"I'm sorry. Is he cheating on you?"

"I…I don't know."

"If he is and we can prove it, we may be able to get around the prenup."

"Uhm. This is a little embarrassing. It wasn't exactly a prenup that I signed."

"What did you sign?"

"Please don't judge me."

"I've known you since college. I've seen you projectile vomit. If I were going to judge you, I would've done it a long time ago."

"True." She smiled. "But this is different."

"I still won't judge you. I wouldn't have gotten through college without you."

"You were a straight A student."

"Only because you helped me with chemistry and

biology. Otherwise, I would've flunked those classes."

"I don't think you would've flunked." But he wouldn't have gotten an A.

"I'm not so sure about that." He laughed and then his tone grew serious. "So what's going on and trust me, I won't judge you."

She took a deep breath. "My marriage isn't a conventional marriage. Harker wants a child."

"It's not uncommon to put stipulations regarding conception in a marriage contract, especially with his amount of money."

"It isn't?"

"Not at all. I see it all the time." His phone beeped. "One second. My mom just texted me." There was a short pause and then he said, "I hate to rush you, but my mom wants me to stop at the store before I go over there for brunch."

"Oh. Right. Uhm." This was so embarrassing. "Harker and I weren't exactly dating when he proposed. And he didn't exactly propose. He suggested that we have a child together. In exchange I'd get to be a partner in his company. Specifically, the software product that I've been working on."

"I assume this is worth a lot of money."

"Yes. A lot."

"Will the two of you stay married? Share custody? What exactly is in this contract?"

"That's the problem. I thought I knew but now I'm not so sure. I do know that we'll stay married until I give birth.

We'll share custody. That's all clear. I thought the rest was too."

"Until…"

"Until he almost broke the contract. Harker would never break a contract. Ever."

"And how did he almost break it?"

"It says that we're to be monogamous until I give birth. Then we'll divorce and I'll get my part of the company."

"And then what?"

"What do you mean?"

"Do you sell your part of the company?"

"No."

"So you'd keep working with your ex. The father of your child?"

"Yeah." Suddenly, it didn't sound as simple as it once had. "We were friends before. We'd go back to being friends again." Okay, now it sounded stupid.

"My experience is that you don't go from being lovers to friends. Some people can but it takes years, but you know your relationship with him better than I do. My info is on my card. Email me the contract and I'll look it over for you. It might take me a couple of days."

"Thank you. I'm sure it's fine but I need to be positive that I didn't miss anything."

"I wish you'd come to me before you signed it."

"Me too."

"I want you to understand that depending on how it's written, there may be something we can do, but probably not much."

"I know." She swallowed. "But I want to know the truth."

"Okay. I'll get back to you as soon as I can."

"Thank you again and Dan?"

"Yeah."

"Make sure you charge me full price."

"Alison, I'm not going to—"

"I insist. Send the bill to Mrs. Augustus Harker."

"Are you sure?"

"Yes. Harker has plenty of money."

"Okay. I'll talk to you soon." He hung up.

Alison stared at the computer, feeling guilty. She shouldn't have done that. She trusted Harker, but something wasn't adding up.

CHAPTER 60: HARKER

Harker had spent most of the day puttering around his office. He'd had a moment of panic after he'd woken and hadn't found Alison in the house. She was angry but he was pretty sure she wouldn't leave. She'd be giving up a lot of money if she did. Still, he'd quietly made his way to her office and had peeked into the room—he refused to think he'd crept. That was creepy. He just didn't want to disturb her. He also refused to think about how once he'd seen her sitting at her computer, he'd been able to breathe again.

He'd gone back to the main part of the house, showered, grabbed something to eat, ran to the store and then had taken a nap. Now, it was almost dinner, and she still wasn't home. Enough was enough. He made his way down the hallway and stepped into her office. "Hey. You hungry?"

Alison jumped, turning toward him. "You scared me."

"Sorry. I didn't mean to." He watched her closely, looking for any sign that she wasn't mad at him anymore. He didn't want to fight with her. He wanted to touch her, kiss her and fuck her, but he'd be happy just holding her…at least for a bit.

"I know you didn't mean to scare me." She didn't smile at him.

"I ordered some groceries."

"You're going to cook?"

"No." He grinned. "I don't want to poison us." He took it as a good sign when she smiled even though it only lasted a second. "I ordered food from the deli. Rotisserie chicken, veggies, rolls. That kind of stuff."

"Sounds good." She turned back to the computer. "Give me a few minutes to finish this up."

"A few minutes? You always say that and then an hour later, I'm back here dragging you away from your desk." He should've walked away but the words had slipped out of his mouth.

"I mean it." She sent him a disgusted look. "I'll be there in ten minutes. I don't lie."

His jaw clenched at her jab. So the war wasn't over. It'd just taken a break. "Please. You've lied numerous times about work, staying a lot longer than you promised."

"That's different."

"You're the one who used it as a comparison."

"Now, I'm un-using it."

"You can't take it back. You said it and I called you on it. You've lied to me about this a lot. A LOT."

"It's not the same and I'm not lying this time."

"I'll wait here because I don't trust you."

"I guess we're in the same boat then." Alison's eyes glistened.

"Fine. I'll be the bigger person in this." He leaned across the desk until his face was only inches from hers. He wanted to shout halleluiah when her eyes dropped to his lips. She must've missed him as much as he missed her. No, that was fucking impossible, but he was glad she missed him at least a little. "I'll trust you. You said ten minutes. I'm giving you ten minutes."

He turned and walked out of the room. He went into the kitchen and started pulling the groceries out of the refrigerator and putting them on the table.

He glanced at his watch when the microwave dinged. It'd been almost fifteen minutes. He was going to drag her out of that office. He headed for the door as she came around the corner, slamming into him. His arms instantly wrapped around her, steadying her, but he didn't let her go. Instead he moved closer, loving the soft press of her body against his.

"Sorry. I almost knocked you down." She stared up at him but didn't try to move away.

"I'm not." He lowered his head. He had to kiss her. It'd been too long since he'd tasted her, felt her breath mingle with his, swallowed her moans as she moved beneath him.

She turned her head and stepped away. He let his arms drop to his side.

"This smells good." She walked to the table and took a seat. "I'm starving."

He sat across from her and they both began filling their plates.

"Thanks for reminding me to eat." She tore off a piece of her roll and popped it into her mouth.

"It's my job to take care of you." He couldn't pull his eyes away from her lips as her tongue darted out to clean off a crumb. He wanted to wrap a biscuit around his dick and let her feast.

"Uh…we need to talk about last night." She took a bite of potato salad.

"Why? Do you want to fight again?"

"No."

"Then let's talk about something else." He buttered his roll.

"Okay. How about the fact that I woke up with you in my bed?"

"Nothing to talk about there. You're my wife and until you're not, we sleep together." He stuffed mashed potatoes into his mouth, not tasting them at all.

"But I didn't want to sleep with you last night."

"We didn't have sex." He took a bite of the chicken. She should be thanking him for that. It hadn't been easy to keep from waking her with his dick.

"That's not the point."

"Oh, it's a bigger point than you understand."

"No, the point is that you lied to me and I'm not sleeping with a man I can't trust."

"Apparently, we're talking about last night."

"No, we're talking about you sneaking into bed with me when you knew I didn't want you there."

"You didn't want me there because you were being

stupid."

"I was not being stupid. You lied to me."

"I did not lie to you." He almost threw his fork down on his plate. "I told you nothing happened and that's exactly what happened. Nothing." He was so sick of this argument.

"Because—"

"It doesn't matter why." He hadn't done a damn thing.

"You're right. All that matters is that you lied to me."

"How did I lie when I told you nothing happened, and nothing happened."

"I asked you to tell me everything that happened."

"Oh, so you wanted to know when I took a piss? And when I scratched my nuts. Did you want to know how fucking blue my balls were because my wife didn't want me."

"Do not start that and don't pretend to be stupid. Almost having sex with your ex-girlfriend is something you should've told me."

"Really? You think I should've told you that?" He slammed his hand down on the table. She must think he was an idiot.

"Yes." Her jaw tightened. She was as angry as he was.

"You were already mad at me."

"For good reason."

"Good reason? I don't see it that way."

"Of course you don't. You wanted to fuck your ex-girlfriend and you're now looking—"

"I *wanted* to fuck my wife." He almost spat the words.

"I'd wanted you for months. Dreamed of fucking you. Sliding inside you. Hearing you moan. Hearing you scream my name. Making you mine and you denied me on our fucking wedding night."

Her eyes widened and she swallowed. "I...I didn't deny you."

"You laughed at me. You thought the idea of me touching you was fucking hysterical." He wanted to throw her on the table and show her how not funny his desire was, but he was too pissed. Angry sex was great, but he wasn't angry, he was furious. If he touched her now, he wouldn't hear her if she said no. So instead, he pushed his chair back and walked across the room. "That night when you found out I'd gone to the Club, I'd finally had a taste of you." He ran his hand through his hair as his eyes locked with hers. "I finally knew what you felt like under me, surrounding me and you were pissed. I wasn't going to tell you anything else that'd ruin this for me...for us. Fuck, Alison. Do you know what it was like wanting you all those months and not being able to touch you? You treated me like a friend." He hated that word. He hated how she'd dismissed him whenever he'd tried to flirt with her. It was as if he were invisible, just like he'd been his entire childhood.

He walked toward her. "I wanted you. I want you." He stopped only a few inches from her. "I want you when I wake, and I want you all day long. You've affected my business, my life. Maybe I should've told you, but I couldn't take the chance that you'd never let me touch you again. But I am swearing to you now, nothing happened. I want you, Alison. No one else."

CHAPTER 61: ALISON

No one had ever spoken to Alison like Harker just did. She'd always been the plain girl, the smart girl, the friend. She'd never been the one the guys fell for and yet, here he was pouring out his…love? No. He hadn't said that. It was more like lust but damn it she was so pathetic even that made her happy. No one had ever lusted after her either, not like this, but what he'd done had hurt. "You still shouldn't have lied."

"I disagree."

"I bet you do." She stood and started for the door. She couldn't make him understand or force him to feel badly about lying to her.

"No, listen." He grabbed her arm and then dropped his hand at her glare. "I wanted you. Telling you something that'd piss you off wouldn't have been smart."

"Hiding it is even dumber because everyone gets caught eventually, including you. If you'd told me everything earlier. I would've been mad, but I would've forgiven you."

"Will you now?"

"I don't know." She didn't usually put up with this kind of stuff from anyone, but everything was different with him. She hated jealous and possessive men, but when he'd acted like that it'd made her insides turn to mush. She sat back down. "Is there anything else Harker? Anything you need to tell me?"

"Yeah, you should kiss me." He smiled sheepishly at her.

"You think this is funny?"

"No. Not at all." His smile disappeared.

"You hurt me. Twice last night."

"I'm sorry."

"But you're not. You don't listen to me."

"I listen to you all the time." He put his hands in his hair and tugged.

"No, you don't. If you did, you wouldn't have snuck into bed with me. You knew I didn't want to be around you."

"We're married. We sleep together. It's that simple."

"It's not simple. If I'm mad and don't want to sleep with you—"

"We're married. We sleep together. I've seen a lot of couples marry and divorce. One of the things I've noticed is that they stop sleeping together for one reason or another. He works late. She fidgets in her sleep. He likes the room cold, and she likes it hot. Whatever the reason, it's bullshit. You and me"—he pointed at her and then himself—"we sleep together."

"Is it in the contract?" She knew it wasn't.

"It should be."

"But it isn't. So that means I don't have to do it."

"Maybe we should say fuck the contract on this issue and decide as a married couple."

"Sounds good. I say I can sleep by myself whenever I want to."

"And I say we sleep together. So we sleep together."

"Excuse me?"

"I'm the man. My vote counts more." His lips turned upward in a silly grin.

Damn him. He was trying to be cute and succeeding. "It so does not. I'm the woman so my vote counts more."

"I would suggest we bet on it but we both know how that'll turn out."

"Yeah, with me winning."

"No, with us fighting."

"Before I win." She gave him a look, daring him to disagree.

He nodded slightly, admitting again that she'd beat him.

"We fight enough. I don't think we need to make our life more difficult.

"I agree. How about you concede on this one and I'll concede on the next?"

"You can't promise that. You don't even know what the next argument will be." She studied him. He was up to something.

"I just did promise it and it doesn't matter. I'll concede. I promise."

"I want that in writing."

"A woman after my own heart." He smiled. "So we agree that we'll concede to every other argument?"

"Only major arguments. Not what we're having for dinner."

His eyes narrowed. "We argue a lot about what we're going to eat."

"Oh my god. That's what you were planning to use as your concession, wasn't it?"

"No. Or at least not until you mentioned it." He smirked. "It would be perfect."

"No. Absolutely not." She laughed. "The concessions have to be over a major issue. A big fight."

"I can argue a lot over food."

"This has to be a fight where we're so mad we don't have sex."

"That's not going to happen again."

"It might if you don't stop being a jerk and lying to me."

"It won't." He stalked toward her. "It shouldn't have happened last night."

"Well, it did, and it might happen tonight too." Although by the wetness between her legs, she'd bet on sex tonight, but she didn't have to let him know that. At least not yet. "I'm not sure I'm ready to let you touch me."

"Really?"

"Yes." Her heart thudded fast and furious as he took that final step toward her.

He towered over her, his dark eyes gleaming with

desire and amusement. "I'll take that as a challenge."

CHAPTER 62: ALISON

"I didn't mean that as a challenge." Alison almost gulped as she stared up at Harker. This was so going to end with them having sex and they both knew it.

"Sounded like one to me." He put his hands on her chair and bent, tipping her backwards.

"Harker," she squeaked, grabbing his shirt.

He lowered his head. "I missed you." His hot breath danced over her lips and then he kissed her.

Her fingers tightened in his shirt and everything disappeared except him. She'd missed him too. She was addicted to the man and how he made her feel—beautiful, wanted, loved. Her heart did a somersault because that's what she wanted, his love.

He deepened the kiss, tipping back her chair a little more and her arms wrapped around his neck. He grabbed her waist, lifting her as the chair crashed to the floor. His hands slid to her ass, pulling her against his body and letting her feel his hardness. His lips traveled up and down her neck, making her shiver and wiggle against him.

"Now, Alison," he whispered in her ear before nipping

her earlobe. "I need you now."

"Yes." She was more than ready for him.

He loosened his hold, letting her slide down his body and feel every hot, hard inch of him. He shoved their dinner out of the way. "Put your hands on the table."

She turned, obeying without hesitation. He unfastened her pants and pushed them and her underwear down to her ankles. He knelt behind her, his hot breath on her ass, his hair tickling her thighs as he lifted her feet and removed her shoes before yanking off her clothes and tossing them aside.

She watched over her shoulder as his focus moved to her butt. He grabbed her thighs, his large hands rough as he pulled them apart before cupping her ass. He kissed along her butt cheeks, licking and nipping where her ass met her thighs. He spread her cheeks, his tongue trailing along the crease and twirling across her butt hole.

"Harker," she gasped. She wasn't sure she was ready for anal play.

He ignored her, his tongue pushing inside her hole. It was wet and hot, and it felt wrong to have his tongue inside her…there. His fingers slid along her pussy, stroking and then he pushed two inside her, his tongue moving deeper into her ass. She gasped, her back arching and pushing her ass and pussy closer to him. His fingers moved faster as his tongue wiggled inside her butt—feeling full and wrong but oh so good.

She moaned as he stood, leaving her wet and aching, empty for him. The sound of his zipper echoed in the quiet room. He stepped closer, one hand on her back pushing her down on the table as his cock slid through her slick folds.

"Harker, please." She wanted him inside her, filling her. She wiggled her butt a little to encourage him.

His hot tip prodded at the entrance to her pussy as he leaned over her, one of his hands clasping hers on the table. His breath tickled her ear as he said, "You want this don't you?" He pushed inside her a little. "Tell me you want this."

She pushed back, taking him in a little deeper. "Yes. Please."

As soon as she said the words, he thrust inside her. She gasped at his intrusion. He was so long and hard. Her body softened, accepting him as he pumped into her in long, hard strokes. He leaned over her, his chest pressing against her back as his other hand grasped hers, fingers tangling.

She moaned, rocking against him as he fucked her. He was as desperate for this as she was. She whimpered as his pace quickened. His body slapped against hers, surrounding her, filling her. Her breasts rubbed along the hard table with each thrust, making her pussy tighten. His arms wrapped around her waist, holding her to his body as his thrusts became faster and shorter. He pressed inward on her abdomen as he pumped faster and faster, his cock stroking her G-spot relentlessly. She wiggled in his grasp, but he held her still, held her close as he pushed her over that cliff, her body stiffening before shattering into a thousand pieces.

He continued fucking her, never letting up on her abdomen. He hit that spot again and again and it was like a fire of electricity. It was too much. Her body trembled as she tried to pull away, but he held her close, forcing her to surrender. That spark of passion tightened and grew, taking over her body until she exploded, screaming as another orgasm rocked through her. He pushed into her again and stilled, groaning as he came before collapsing on top of her, his breath rough and ragged in her ear. She felt wonderful, boneless, but too soon reality returned. The table was hard especially with his weight on top of her.

"Harker." She shifted under him.

"Oh. Yeah." He stood, lifting her with him as he grabbed a chair and sat, pulling her onto his lap. He trailed featherlike kisses along her neck and shoulder.

She relaxed against him. She could stay like this forever—his strong arms around her and his dick still buried inside her.

"Forgive me Alison." He kissed her ear.

"Always." She turned and kissed him. She loved him too much to do anything else.

CHAPTER 63: ALISON

Alison sat in her office, daydreaming. The last few days had been better than wonderful. After work she and Harker would have dinner and watch TV or talk. She'd snuggle against his side, listening to his heartbeat. Other nights, they'd lie in bed and watch porn. Once she'd even read some kinky romance stories to him. She shivered at the memory. Harker was always good in bed but that night he'd been...inspired. She'd barely been able to walk the next day. His cocky smirk every time he'd see her wince when she sat made her want to slap him and kiss him senseless.

Alison's phone rang and her stomach twisted as bile rose in her throat. She put her head between her legs and took deep breaths until her nausea eased. Her phone stopped ringing and then it beeped. She forced herself to look at the screen and she almost sank into her chair. It'd been Ellie not Dan.

She should've never asked him to look over the contract. Harker would be so hurt if he knew she hadn't trusted him. It was too late anyway. She'd signed it already.

She should call Dan and tell him to forget it but whenever she picked up the phone something stopped her.

Every day, she'd spend hours convincing herself that Harker would respect this decision. He'd told her to get a lawyer before she'd signed the contract. What difference did it make if she did it now? Then every time her phone rang or beeped, she'd panic, knowing that no matter what she told herself this would hurt him deeply. She may not have had a reason to trust him before, but she should trust him now. It wasn't worth ruining whatever was happening between them. She picked up her phone. She was calling Dan.

"Alison, get in here," bellowed Harker from down the hall.

"Maybe we should've kept playing that game," she mumbled to herself as she dropped her phone on her desk and pressed the button for Harker's Barker-Meter. She burst out laughing when it spit out, *Alison, get in here now.* "Close enough." She stood and headed to Harker's office.

He sat behind his desk, glaring at his computer.

She tapped on the door. "You bellowed, my lord?"

He looked up, his dark eyes hot. "Come here. And close the door behind you."

Her body melted at the look in his eyes and the promise in his voice. She stepped inside, shutting the door but didn't move any closer. They'd had sex in his office before but usually it was later in the day. They always quit early and went home because a quick wham-bam wasn't ever enough for him.

"I said come here." He pushed back from his desk.

"Harker, I have a lot of work to do."

"I don't care." He stood.

Her eyes skimmed down his body. His dick was already tenting his pants. She bit her lip, unable to pull her gaze away from his cock. "It's not even ten o'clock." She lowered her voice. "We just had sex."

"Who said anything about sex?"

Her eyes darted up to his. "Oh…" She flushed. "It's just that"—she waved her hand at his erection—"and your tone. It's the same when we're…in the bedroom and…"

"Take off your clothes, Alison." He unhooked his belt and her knees actually knocked together.

She'd didn't hesitate as she pulled off her shirt. She'd learned to love a man with a belt in his hands.

CHAPTER 64: HARKER

Alison shimmied out of her underwear and Harker's dick grew even harder as he saw the wetness glistening in the curls between her legs.

"Hold out your hands." His cock almost exploded when she obeyed without hesitation. He wrapped his belt around her wrists and tightened it. "Now, you're mine."

"I was yours the second I heard that tone in your voice." Her eyes were dark and heavy with desire.

"Prove it. Get on your knees." He took her arm, helping her to kneel before him. "Open your mouth and look at me."

She stared up at him, her pink tongue slipping out to wet her bottom lip. He unzipped his pants, pulling out his cock and tapping it against her cheek. His precum glistened on her face.

"Stick out your tongue." When she did, he slapped his dick against it, loving the hot wetness that teased his sensitive tip. "That's it." He slid inside her mouth and she closed around him, sucking. "Fuck. Yes." He clasped her hair, tangling it in his fist as she sucked him, bobbing up and down on his cock. Her mouth felt fucking perfect. "Look at me."

Her eyes raised to his as his cock disappeared past her lips. His fist tightened in her hair as he began to pump into her. With her hands tied and him holding her in place she was at his mercy but there was no fear or doubt in her eyes—only excitement.

He'd die before he hurt her, but he would push her past comfort and into pleasure. She pressed forward and his cock slid into her throat. He wanted to fuck her face but instead he dropped his hand from her head, giving her control. He groaned as she sucked him deeper, her throat squeezing his dick for one exquisite moment before she pulled off him and coughed.

"You good?" Because he wanted back inside that mouth. He ran his hand over her cheek.

"Yes." Her voice was raspy–from desire or his cock scraping her throat he wasn't sure and didn't care.

"Again." His thumb traced her lower lip and she sucked it, letting her teeth graze his skin.

He grabbed his dick and she opened, her tongue twirling around the top before sucking that sensitive tip into her mouth. She sucked hard, rubbing her tongue against him, making his balls tighten and his hips thrust. She opened wider as she moved forward, his cock sliding deep into her throat. He groaned, his fists clenching at his sides. He should pull out. Fill her pussy with his cum but she felt so fucking good as she sucked him harder. Her bound hands lifted, cupping his balls and squeezing gently.

"Fuck." He grabbed her head and pulled her off his cock. He lifted her to her feet and into his arms. "As soon as you tell me you're pregnant, I'm going to fuck that mouth of yours until I come down your throat and you're going to swallow every bit."

CHAPTER 65: ALISON

Alison wrapped her legs around Harker's waist as he kissed her, his tongue taking her mouth. She rubbed her pussy along his hard cock, pressing it against her clit.

"Oh, no." Harker grabbed her waist and pulled her away from his cock.

"What's the matter?" She put her bound hands on his chest, loving the way his heart raced. He'd been close to coming in her mouth. All he needed was a little incentive and he'd be inside her in a second. She kissed along his neck, licking and sucking.

"What's the matter?" He took two steps to his desk and dropped her onto it, undoing his belt from around her wrists and tossing it aside.

She tightened her legs, not ready to let him go.

"You. You're what's the matter." He pried her legs from his waist. "I need you." He grabbed her face between his two large hands.

"You can have me," she whispered.

"Don't tempt me." His eyes darkened and he kissed her. It was hard and a little desperate. "I need you as horny as I am because when I fuck you, it's going to be hard and fast."

"I'm ready." At least she thought she was.

"Not even close." He smiled wickedly. "But you will be." He grabbed one of the chairs and sat, grasping her thighs and spreading her legs wide. "You have the prettiest pussy." He ran one finger along her slit. "So slick and pink and"—he slid the finger inside her, her body clenching around him—"so fucking needy."

He bent kissing her legs. She leaned back on her elbows, watching his dark head slowly making its way between her thighs.

He pulled her forward until she balanced on the edge of the desk as his hot breath whispered across her swollen pussy lips. He spread her open and licked up and down in long strokes, his tongue flat pushing hard on her sensitive flesh.

"Oh, god." Her head dropped back onto her shoulders. "That feels…so…good." Her hips began to move as he licked her, back and forth, over and over.

Her legs tried to squeeze shut to keep him close, but his fingers dug into her thighs, spreading her even wider. He gave her one more long lick before flicking his tongue side to side, teasing her clit and sending pleasure soaring through her.

"Oh…yes…that's. Oh, Harker." Her body tightened, getting ready to come but he switched his kiss again. This time his tongue rolled in circles over her tiny bud that swelled almost painfully with need. Her arms shook and she dropped onto the desk unable to hold herself up any longer. Her fingers slid through his hair as her hips rocked, trying to find release.

He stood, wiping his face with the back of his hand before pulling her almost off the desk as he stepped between her thighs. The head of his cock was purple and dripping. His eyes met hers as he thrust inside her.

She gasped as he filled her, but he didn't even pause. He lifted her legs to his hips, his hand cupping her throat as he fucked her, hard and fast, barely leaving her body. He reached between them, his thumb finding her clit and rubbing hard.

"Harker…wait…ouch…that's…too much." Pain shot through her from where he rubbed. It was hot and intense and then it sparked into something more as he fucked her faster.

His body slapped against hers, his thumb mercilessly pressing on her clit. Sensations intense and wild exploded throughout her body. Her legs dropped from his waist as she squirmed, both trying to get away and trying to rub against him. His hand moved from her throat, pressing down between her breasts, pinning her beneath him.

"Let go, Alison. Fucking let go." He kissed her, rough and desperate as his hips lost all rhythm and he groaned into her mouth.

She wiggled under him but there was no escape as he pounded into her, hard and fast, His thumb continued to rub on her clit as his mouth devoured hers. She was nothing but feelings—pressure, pain, pleasure—all tangled together.

Her body bucked, trying to get away but her movements shoved him deeper, and she screamed, her body shaking as she came. He grunted, slamming into her a few more times before he found his release.

His thrusts slowed and finally subsided. He kissed her shoulder. "Fuck. We need to do this every day."

"We already do." She kissed his neck, her body boneless. "At least every night and every morning."

"Yes, but I meant during work. We'll try the chairs next time." He smiled against her neck. "We'll call it our fuck break. It'll be a company thing."

"Oh, we shouldn't."

"That wasn't a no." He kissed her quickly before stepping back and pulling up his pants. "I'll never look at my desk the same way." His eyes heated again as his gaze wandered over her. "If you plan on getting any work done today, you'd better get dressed fast. You look too fucking hot spread wide open and naked on my desk with my cum dripping from your pussy." His eyes heated again.

"Oh. No. Quit looking at me like that." She jumped off the desk and hurried around him, gathering her clothes. "I'm already way behind."

"Is Mac slacking?"

"No. Not at all." She pulled on her panties. "But he's still in school and only works part-time." She put on her bra. "Soon he'll be fulltime, and we'll catch up. He's doing great." She grabbed her shirt and pants, sliding them on.

"Great? Hmmm. Who said you should hire him?"

"You." She forced the word out of her mouth. The man

was too cocky as it was.

"You know, you're a boss now. You should reward people for good work…or good suggestions."

"It wasn't a suggestion. You hired him."

He frowned. "The particulars don't matter. I was right, and I should be rewarded."

"You're lucky I forgave you for that."

He walked over to her and kissed her. "I am that and I'm lucky you were greedy enough to agree to my baby deal." He wrapped his arms around her waist, his hands resting on her ass.

"That's true. I almost didn't." She leaned into him, wishing it was after work and they could talk and cuddle.

"I would've figured out something." He kissed her gently. "I'd wanted you for too long to let you slip away."

"Oh, Harker." She touched his cheek, her heart melting at his confession.

CHAPTER 66: ALISON

Alison walked into her office, a warm glow filling her and it was from more than her orgasm, not that it hadn't been great. She absolutely loved sex with Harker. She'd always enjoyed sex but with him it was different—exciting, fun, super-hot and something else, something deeper.

She sighed as she dropped onto her chair, opening her laptop. She needed to get her head back into her program, but all she wanted to do was to crawl onto Harker's lap and stay there. Her phone rang and she grabbed it.

"Hey, Ellie. Sorry I didn't—"

"Hey, Alison. It's Dan."

The bile rose in her throat.

"Sorry it took me so long to get back with you, but I was—"

"It's not a problem. I was going to call you and tell you not to bother."

"Oh." He paused. "I think you should hear what I found."

Her stomach twisted and she swallowed, trying hard not to vomit.

"Alison? Are you still there?"

"I'm not sure I want to know," she whispered.

"I think you should." His voice was calm. This was Dan, the one guy all women trusted.

"Okay." Whatever it was, she could handle it.

"You were right about the monogamy clause. It does state that both parties have to be monogamous."

"Oh, thank God." She slid down on her seat. "I read that clause so many times. I knew what it said but there was something about the way he was acting. Maybe I am pregnant." She swallowed again. Now that she thought about it, she might be late. Her periods had never been regular, but she was...How many days late was she?

"Hold on. I'm not done. There are addendums to this contract. A lot of them."

"Yeah. I read them too." Those hadn't made much sense to her. Just lots of lawyer-speak.

"I haven't had a chance to look through all of it, but I did find one that referred to what I call the monogamy clause."

"And." Cold sweat broke out across her skin.

"And it says..." Dan started reading.

"Stop. Please. I don't understand a word you're saying. Tell me what it says in English." Her hand squeezed the phone so tight her fingers ached.

"Okay. This addendum states that the monogamy clause only pertains to those individuals whose parentage is not in question."

"I don't understand. That's still not English."

"Okay. Basically, for a woman parentage is never in question. If she's pregnant, it's always her kid, baring surrogates. For a man, parentage is always in question."

"So you're saying that because I know it'll be my child that I have to be monogamous, but he doesn't?"

"I'm not saying it, the addendum is, but yes. You have to be monogamous so that he knows the child is his. He doesn't have to be monogamous because you will always know the child you carry is yours. It kind of makes sense."

"That bastard."

"Uh…Yeah. From a legal view it's brilliant but from a personal view…That bastard."

"I'm going to kill him."

"Hold off on that."

"Why?" She was furious.

"Because there's a lot more to this contract. I'll use non-lawyer terms. This thing is slippery. Do you want me to keep looking into it to see what else is hidden in all those addendums?"

"Yeah. Read it all. I need to know everything."

"Okay, but do you care if I show it to my boss because some of this is beyond my experience. Whoever wrote this is freaking brilliant."

"Lucky them." She wanted to strangle that person too. "And yeah, show it to whomever you need to. Just find out what exactly I signed." She hung up the phone and stood. It was time to wring Harker's lying neck.

CHAPTER 67: HARKER

Harker looked up from his computer as Alison walked into his office. "Ready for round two?" He closed his laptop. "It'll have to be quick. I have a meeting in"—he glanced at his watch—"about twenty minutes."

"I'm not here to have sex with you." She stopped in front of his desk.

"You sure about that?" He had no idea why she was so pissed. He hadn't done anything since he'd fucked-her-happy a little while ago, so it was probably the code she was working on. "I can help you release that tension in a much more enjoyable way."

"Don't be a smart-ass. I had a lawyer look over the contract."

Apparently, it *was* him. Now, he had to wait and see which part of the contract had her so upset.

"You never had any intention of being monogamous."

So, that was it. That one was easy. "Alison, I've been faithful, and you know it."

"I don't know anything. I didn't know you went to the Club on our wedding night, and I didn't know you almost fucked your ex-sub. I thought I could trust you, but according to my lawyer, I was wrong about that too."

"Generally, people have their lawyer look at contracts before they sign them." He had no idea why she was upset. She'd signed it weeks ago. There was nothing she could do about it now.

"Yeah well, I trusted you."

"That was your mistake." He grinned.

"It's not funny Harker."

"How can you be upset about this? You know I haven't been with anyone but you and I have every intention of staying monogamous." He stood and walked over toward her. "I want *you,* Alison. No one else."

"Then why did you put that addendum in the contract if you didn't want to have sex with other women?"

"We wrote the contract before I knew how it'd be with you." He half-sat on his desk, taking her hands to pull her into his arms.

She pushed him away and took a step back. "So, if you hadn't been satisfied with how I was in bed, you'd be out fucking other women."

"Yeah." He shrugged.

"You son of a bitch."

"Oh come on. If it wasn't good for me, it wouldn't be good for you either. You'd be happy I wasn't panting after you and pestering you to have unsatisfying sex morning, noon and night." He grinned. "You know how much I want sex." Although, he wanted it with her more than with any other woman he'd ever met.

"You're saying this was for my benefit?"

"In a way, yeah. It would've saved us both some hassles but only if we weren't compatible. Normally, we would've dated and fucked before marriage. This was protection for both of us."

"Sounds more like a prison sentence for me. I'd have to put up with your ineptitude in bed, but you'd get to fuck anyone you wanted. If you were really looking out for both of us, I'd get to find someone better to fuck too."

"That isn't possible. The entire point of the contract was me having a child. There's no doubt that it'll be your child. There's no reason for me to have to be monogamous but it's necessary that you only have sex with me until you conceive."

"Too bad I'm not pregnant now because then I could go out and fuck the first guy I see."

"That's not going to happen. Sex between us is great so there's no reason for either of us to seek out anyone else." He'd tie her to his bed if she tried. She was his. His wife. His lover. His.

"If there's no reason for the addendum to the clause, change it."

"Since I have no intention of sleeping with anyone else that part of the contract doesn't matter."

"It does to me."

"It shouldn't. We're together all the time."

"Now, but what about later? If you decide to have sex with somebody else you don't lose the baby, but if I do sleep with someone besides you, I lose my partnership in the company."

"That's not true. If you have sex with someone else, that puts my part of the contract at risk. You could be pregnant with somebody else's child and I wouldn't know that until we had a DNA test after the baby was born."

"Harker just change the contract. If we're married, we both—"

"If we're married?" He wanted to punch something every time she pointed out that their marriage wasn't real. "Oh, that's right. We're only married for the contract as you like to point out. The contract that you read and signed as it is right now."

"Why is this such a big deal to you? If you don't plan on having sex with anyone else, then change the contract. Otherwise, I have to assume that you're planning to do exactly that."

"I am not. I don't want anyone else, and you should trust me. Every relationship is built on trust. Other couples don't have contracts. If they're together they're monogamous, and that's how I feel about you. About us. I'm with you. I'm not going to be with anyone else."

"But we do have a contract and you put in writing that you get to fuck anyone you want."

"Because you'll know it's your baby. I won't."

"But you should trust me Harker," she said sweetly, throwing his words back at him.

"I do trust you," he said through clenched teeth.

"Then remove the monogamy part altogether so it's just you and me and whatever"—she waved her hand between them—"this is."

"How can I do that when you won't even call it a relationship?"

"Fine. It's a relationship."

"You don't mean that." And the truth of that tore him up. "You still think of this as a business deal. Since that's the case, then I'd be an idiot to change the contract. You read it. You signed it. It stands as is. Perhaps you should've taken my advice and hired a lawyer before you signed it."

"You're unbelievable." She stormed to the door but stopped, turning back toward him. "This isn't over. You want to play this game, we can play. I'm not one of those subservient idiots you usually date. I like to think for myself." She walked away, slamming the door behind her.

"And that's why I picked you to have my baby," he yelled. "I don't want a stupid kid."

CHAPTER 68: ALISON

Alison stared at the computer screen, too angry to think straight let alone work. Harker was being a colossal jerk. There was no reason for him to keep that addendum in the contract unless he wanted to have an affair. No, not an affair because none of this was real—not their marriage, not their relationship and not even the way she felt for him. It was all pretend. She just had to convince her heart about that.

Mac strolled into the room, dropping his backpack on the floor by his desk.

"You're early." It wasn't even lunchtime yet.

"Yeah, one of my professors is sick." His brow wrinkled. "You having a problem with the code?"

She almost said yes. That would've been the easy answer except it wouldn't work with Mac. He'd offer to help. "No."

"Oh." He looked at her oddly, as if computer problems were the only ones in the world. At his age, that was probably true. "Then what's the matter?"

"Personal problems." Like being married to an ass who

she'd fallen in love with but who had permission in writing to cheat on her.

"Oh." Now, the poor kid looked like he was ready to run from the room. "Is there something…Do you want to talk?"

She did but not with Mac. It wouldn't be fair to put him in the middle of her and Harker. "No. Thanks any—"

"Great. I mean, not great but…"

"It's fine."

He nodded and sat at his deck, pulling out his laptop and hooking it to the system. His fingers flew over the keyboard and he got a focused look on his face. He was gone from this horrible reality and living in code-land.

She envied him. He had nothing to worry about but grades and finishing a project. She'd thought those days were so complicated, but they were nothing compared to her life now. She looked back at her computer, but it was no use. She couldn't concentrate. She stood, closing her laptop. "I'm going to go home for the day."

He grunted something, not even looking up from his computer. She headed toward the house. The door to Harker's office was open. She paused. She'd been hoping he'd left it closed, but whatever. She wasn't hiding from him. He was the one who was wrong. She walked by.

"Alison," he said.

She stopped, glancing into his office. "What?"

"Where are you going?"

"I'm done for the day."

"Are you feeling okay?" He got up, walking toward

her.

"I'm fine or I would be if you'd change the contract."

"That's not a reason to leave work early."

"Being sick is."

"You said you were fine."

"I am, but I'm also sick of you."

"Alison, I'm not going to sleep with anyone else." He sounded as exasperated as she felt.

"Then it shouldn't bother you to change the contract."

"I made my reasons perfectly clear."

"You've made everything perfectly clear and that's great because now I get to make it crystal clear how I feel about it." She was going to make him see her side of this if it killed her.

"Go ahead, Alison. Get back at me. Don't let me touch you. It won't last long. You like sex as much as I do." He grinned. "Well, maybe not quite as much as I do." He moved closer to her. "I just have to decide which will be more fun. Seducing you or waiting until you can't take it anymore and letting you jump me."

"That is never going to happen." She turned and walked down the hallway, pulling her phone from her pocket. She dialed Ellie. She needed a friend's shoulder to cry on and a partner in crime.

"Hey Alison," said Ellie.

"Do you want to go out tonight? Later. After work?" She walked into the living room and flopped on the couch.

"Oh, I can't. Adrian is having some of the guys over. They're watching an MMA fight."

"One of Marc's fights?" She couldn't believe Ellie would want to watch her ex, unless he was going to get his ass kicked.

"No. Not Marc." Ellie laughed. "There's no way I'd let Adrian watch that here. I'd probably bash the TV with a bat as soon as I saw the bastard."

"I was wondering." Their breakup hadn't been amicable.

"Do you and Harker want to come over here? Adrian ordered plenty of food."

"I'm not going anywhere with Harker."

"Uh-oh. What happened?"

"Do you have an hour?" It'd take a least that long for her to get out her frustrations.

"No. Can you give me the abridged version now and the longer one later?"

"I thought you couldn't go out."

"I thought you wanted to double-date but since it's just you and me, I can definitely go. So what happened?" asked Ellie.

"The short version is that I didn't understand the contract and the only one who has to be monogamous is me."

"What? It's actually in the contract that he can sleep with other women, but you can't have sex with other men?"

"Yeah, and he refuses to change it. He says that other couples don't need a contract to be faithful and that he has no intention of having sex with anyone else."

"Don't let him give you that shit. He may not be

planning it exactly but he's leaving that option open. Men can be such lying, cheating assholes."

"I know." Alison felt vindicated. If Ellie agreed with her then she wasn't being unreasonable. It didn't matter that Ellie had a lot to say about cheaters because every one of her boyfriends before Adrian had cheated on her.

"Men will make excuses for everything," continued Ellie. "One of my exes actually argued that he hadn't cheated because they'd only had oral sex. Can you believe that?"

"Oh…" Alison stood. "That's it."

"I know that tone," said Ellie. "That big brain of yours is working overtime. I have to tell you, I'm both terrified and fascinated. What are you going to do?"

"I'll explain everything tonight. Right now, I have to get ready. I'm going shopping. I need a new outfit."

"Oh…I'm so excited. Where do you want to meet?"

"Murphy's. We can get something to eat. I'm in the mood for some fried, greasy, fatty foods. We'll eat, I'll tell you everything and then we'll go out clubbing."

CHAPTER 69: HARKER

Harker closed his computer. It was late. Time to go face the wrath that was Alison. He still hadn't decided if he should seduce her or wait. They both had merits. He walked down the hallway toward his house.

He loved the slow art of seduction—the seemingly accidental touches of his hand and body against hers, the covert looks that lasted only long enough for her to notice, the double entendres and dance of words. It was mental foreplay that could last for hours and lead to mind-blowing sex.

However, while he wasn't a fan of abstinence, this time waiting might be worth it. Alison would hold out, fighting her desire, until she was creaming her panties when he looked in her direction. That would mean when they finally did fuck, it'd be rough, hard and desperate.

The question was how long would he have to wait? If he seduced her, he'd have sex tonight. That was a big plus. He wasn't in the mood to wait days. He needed to gauge exactly how angry she was—one day mad or one week mad. He'd be willing to wait a day or two for a night of hard, selfish fucking but a week? No way.

He walked into his house. Alison wasn't in the living room. He headed toward the bedroom, the faint hint of perfume making his balls tighten. Maybe she wasn't angry at all anymore.

He stepped into the doorway and his dick about punched a hole through his pants. Alison wore a slinky black dress that he'd never seen, and he knew that for sure because he'd remember that dress on his deathbed.

She had one foot on the bed, pulling sheer black stockings up her long, shapely leg. She glanced at him as she put her foot down and slid it into a sexy, black high-heeled shoe before putting her other foot on the bed.

His eyes roamed over her. The dress looked like a slip and it hugged her ass and scooped down at the front. If she bent, he'd be able to see her breasts. If this was any other day, he'd tell her to bend because he really wanted to see her tits. Instead, he said, "I hadn't expected this but I'm definitely not disappointed." He leaned against the doorframe to stop himself from charging into the room and throwing her on the bed. "You look amazing. I don't think I'll be able to make it through dinner without tearing your clothes off with my teeth."

"I'm sure you'll make it through dinner and longer." She put her leg down, slipping on her other shoe before walking into the bathroom.

He followed as if on a leash, stopping in the doorway. His dick grew another inch as she picked up a tube of lipstick and opened her mouth wide before sliding that phallic shaped gloss all over her lips.

That was it. His control snapped. "Fuck dinner. We're not even going to make it out of the bathroom." He took a step, ready to grab her, drop her sexy ass on the sink and slide into her so deep she screamed.

She spun toward him. "Don't touch me. You lost that right."

"Oh. I get it." He hated this game, but he'd play, and he'd win. "You're going to get all dressed up in clothes that scream *please fuck me* but not let me touch you until I change the contract." He leaned against the wall, to make sure he didn't reach for her. "Well my dear, it's not going to work. I'm more stubborn than you are, and I'll win this game."

"I'm not playing a game." She dropped the lipstick in her purse. "You're not touching me until I know for sure I'm not pregnant."

"Are you pregnant?" Excitement raced through him. "Do you need to sit? Are you hungry?" He wanted to hug her, hold her, protect her.

"I don't know, but I could be. Until I do know or you change that contract, we aren't having sex."

He wasn't one to be threatened. "If you break the contract, you lose everything." He stalked toward her. "Your job. Your program. Everything."

"I have no intention of breaking the contract."

"And how do you expect to get pregnant if we don't have sex?"

"I may be pregnant."

"Possibly." He moved closer. His eyes darted to her throat where her pulse beat erratically. He'd trained her well. She may hate him right now, but her body wanted his. "But if not, you will have to have sex with me."

"Yes, after my period we'll have sex." Her body swayed toward him.

He fought a grin. She was so close if she took a deep breath her tits would rub against his chest.

"Once. And then a month later, once again, until I am pregnant."

"Once a month?" That was not happening. He needed sex a lot more than that and even though he could fuck someone else he didn't want to. Right now, he was too fascinated by her.

"Yes. Once is all it takes. Don't worry. I checked with my lawyer to make sure it wouldn't violate the contract."

"You should hire a better lawyer. The contract clearly states that you can't refuse to have sex with me." He smiled softly. "I should stop being so lenient about that clause."

"It does state that but there is no reason for me to engage in relations with you once I'm pregnant."

"You don't know that you're pregnant." A cold chill ran down his spine. He'd helped to engineer enough loopholes in contracts to recognize one when he heard it.

"And I don't know that I'm not." She touched her breasts, squeezing. "These are a bit tender. It could be because I'm expecting, or it could be my period is on its way." She shrugged. "We won't know until I either have my period or don't."

She was right. He was going to have a word with his lawyer about this oversight. "Okay. Think of it this way, the more often we fuck the sooner you can be done with me."

"Trust me, that is appealing but I don't think I could stand to let you touch me more than once a month. I despise cheaters."

"I'm not cheating." He almost shouted and then took a deep breath. "And I have no intention of fucking anyone but you."

"Then change the contract." Her jaw jutted out stubbornly, but he was the king of stubborn.

"You should trust me."

"I did until I realized you screwed me in the contract."

"I didn't screw you. I had no idea what sex would be like between us. I'd hoped it'd be good, but I wasn't condemning myself to shitty sex for months."

"But you had no problem condemning me to shitty sex."

"You can't have sex with anyone else. It's the only way I'll know the baby is mine. Don't say I can have a DNA test done because I'm well aware of that, but I'd have to wait months. Your monogamy was the only way."

"And the only way we're going to have sex more than once a month is if you revise the contract."

"I'm not doing that."

"Then enjoy sex once a month."

"I think you've forgotten that I can have sex as often as I like." He took her hand in his. "While you, my dear, can only have it once a month." His thumb traced across her skin. "Do you think you can handle that? You like sex almost as much as I do."

"Almost?"

"Yes." His gaze met hers and the sharp glint in her eyes almost made his balls tuck back into his body, but he kept going. He could talk her out of being mad at him; he'd done it before. "If you liked it as much as me, we'd be fucking right now, not talking." He put her hand on his dick which was hard and ready to go.

"You're right." She squeezed his cock.

"That's what I like to hear." He rested his hand on her ass, pulling her closer.

"I may not like sex as much as you, but I do like orgasms."

"I know. Let's go have a few. We'll see if we can beat our record."

"No." She stepped back, and he swore his dick grew trying to reach her hand. "I don't need you for those."

He wasn't giving up yet. "Masturbatory orgasms are never as good as the ones I can give you."

"Who's talking about masturbation?" She left the bathroom and walked into the living room.

"You are." He followed her, a little tornado forming in his gut. She was up to something. "You can't fuck anyone but me."

"Who said anything about fucking?" She headed toward the door.

"Where are you going?"

"To find a man to give me an orgasm." She ran her hands over her breast. "I have to admit I'm extremely horny right now."

"What the fuck are you talking about?" That little tornado was now a hurricane.

"There's nothing in the contract about oral." She smiled and then pursed her lips. "Or anal but I'm not sure I'll have an orgasm from that." She pulled her keys from her purse. "It doesn't matter. I can decide if I want to do anal at any time."

"No. Those are considered sex and that means the only person you can do them with is me." He slapped his chest like a pissed off gorilla, and it wasn't too far from the way he felt.

"You're wrong. The contract specifically talks about intercourse. Vaginal sex."

"It doesn't specify. It states that you can't have sex with anyone but me. Period."

"But only as it pertains to me getting pregnant. Sex that could result in pregnancy is the only kind I have to have with you. Don't worry." She smiled. "I double checked with my lawyer." She took a step toward him. "Just think. All those blow jobs you love, you're going to have to get them from someone else because these lips"—she ran her finger over her mouth, letting it slip inside where his dick wanted to be—"are never going to wrap around your cock again but they are going to find some other dick to suck. Don't worry. I'll make sure that there's no vaginal penetration by a penis, but tongue and fingers are a different story." She smiled, her eyes sparkling with triumph. "Have a nice evening."

"No." It was the only word that his brain could form. "No," he repeated.

"Yes." She walked toward the door. "I'm used to at least one orgasm a night and I have no intention of going back to being celibate. You've taught me so much." She reached for the doorknob.

Harker didn't think. His mind filled with images of Alison on her knees, surrounded by men. Pricks all around her and he exploded across the room, his shoulder hitting the door and knocking her to the side.

"Move." She grabbed the door handle.

"No way in hell." He pressed his back against the door.

"I'm serious. Get out of my way."

"No," he growled.

"You know, this is kidnapping."

"Call the cops. I'll explain to them how my wife wants to go out and suck some strange guy's dick and not one of them will blame me for not letting you leave."

"You are such an asshole." She turned and started for the bedroom and then stopped, heading toward the business part of the mansion.

"Work as late as you want, Alison, but remember you sleep with me tonight. We agreed to that."

"Go to hell, Harker."

"As I told you before, I have an express pass since marrying you."

CHAPTER 70: HARKER

Harker checked his watch. It'd been several hours since their fight. Alison had to be hungry. He was starving, and he'd already eaten a sandwich. It'd been really good. He could eat another one. That was it. He'd make them both a sandwich and take it to her as a peace offering. They could eat and talk and then maybe go to bed.

He went into the kitchen and pulled out the packages of meat and cheese. He took out four slices of bread and then grabbed the mustard and mayonnaise. He paused. A couple of days ago she'd said the mayo had upset her stomach, but he'd seen her eat it with tomatoes yesterday. He should ask her what she wanted on her sandwich. If he didn't, she'd probably bitch about how he never paid attention. He didn't need to give her another reason to be mad at him.

He put the condiments on the counter and walked into the office. The hallway was dark. The only light came from the kitchen and Alison's office. He tapped on the open door and stepped inside. Mac was alone in the room.

"Oh. Hey." His gaze went to Alison's desk.

"Hey, Harker." Mac glanced up at him and then back to the computer.

"Is she in the restroom?" Maybe she was getting ready to come home. Her laptop was closed and there was no bottle of water on her desk like there usually was.

"Who?" asked Mac.

"Alison."

"I don't know."

"You don't know where she went?"

"She said she was going home."

"When was this?" His brain sounded an alarm bell. He should've seen her in the hallway.

"Hours ago. Right after I got here."

"But you did see her again this evening, right?"

Mac looked up at him, frowning in thought. "No, but I don't pay too much attention to anything else when I'm working." His face brightened. "It's going great. I broke through the AI's refusal to recognize—"

"You're saying that she didn't come back here this evening. She would've been dressed up. In a dress. There's no way you wouldn't have noticed her." The kid might be a geek, but he was still male.

"I haven't seen her since right before lunch."

"Fuck."

"Is everything okay, Mr. Harker?"

"No, but I'll handle it. Go back to work." He raced down the hallway to the employees' entrance. He burst into the garage where the staff parked and ran to the door to his personal garage. He punched in his keycode and stepped inside. Alison's car was gone.

Fuck. He hated smart women. He grabbed his phone and ran back to the house. His call went straight to voicemail and he almost slammed his phone against the wall when he heard the message.

Hi, sorry I can't get to the phone right now. Leave a message unless you're Harker. Then don't bother. Just go to hell but before you do that, I want you to know that I'm having a really, really good time.

He hung up and dialed Ellie's number. It also went straight to voicemail.

Hi, this is Ellie. Leave a message. If you're Harker don't bother unless you're calling to say that you changed the contract. Then leave a message and I'll see if I can pull Alison away from all the fun we're having.

"You two think you're so fucking funny," he shouted at the phone. "You're not. You're not funny at all." He dialed Adrian's number.

"Hey Harker, what's up." The TV blared in the background and it sounded like there was a crowd.

"Where are you?"

"Home."

"Oh…the noise."

"Watching the fight."

"Where's Ellie? Where did she and Alison go?"

"I can't tell you that."

"What?" If his phone made it through the night without being smashed, he'd be surprised.

"If I tell you, I'll be in as much shit as you're in and I don't want to sleep on the couch."

"Adrian, I'm not fucking around. Tell me where they went." The guy thought everything was a fucking joke.

"I'm not either. Ellie specifically told me...Actually, she told me not to answer your call, but I felt bad for you. The bro code, you know."

"Not much of a code if you won't help me."

The guys shouted in the background.

"Hold on a second," said Adrian.

Harker paced. He had to find her before she did something stupid.

"Harker." Adrian must've gone into another room because it was a lot quieter. "Ellie told me what's going on. Change the contract, dude. It ain't worth the fight."

"I'm not going to sleep with anyone else so there's no reason to change the contract. She should trust me."

"It'll make her happy, Harker. That's reason enough."

He started to protest but paused. Adrian had a point but damn it, so did he.

"If you would've agreed to change the contract, she'd be there with you now. Is it worth all this if you're not planning on fucking someone else?"

"I'll think about it. Now, where are they?"

"Seriously man, I can't tell you that."

"So you answered the phone to give me advice?" He wanted to punch the guy. "Why the fuck would I want advice from you?"

"Okay. I won't take that personally because I know how pissed off you are right now. I'd be climbing the rafters if Ellie was out looking for…uh…something. Actually, I'd be checking every club, restaurant, bar in the area."

"I thought I'd try getting help from a friend first." They weren't exactly friends, but he'd use whatever he could to get information. "But I shouldn't have bothered. I'm on my way to check every place in the city."

"Before you do that, listen to me. I've been in the PI/security business for a little while now and women who want to cheat don't tell their husbands."

"They do if they want revenge." He headed for his car.

"No, most still don't tell their husbands but if they do it's after the fact."

"Great. Alison is special. I've known that for a long time."

"You're not listening to me. What I'm saying is Alison doesn't want to do this."

"Right. I'm forcing her to suck some guy's dick."

"Fucking-A, you're a thick-headed bastard. I'm not saying that."

"Then you'd better speak very clearly because that's what I'm hearing."

"What I'm saying is she's not going to do anything tonight. Keep this up and she might, but she's not the kind of woman to pick up a strange guy at a club or a bar."

"She might to get back at me." He couldn't forget how she'd been with Ethan, writhing and clutching him to her breast. If she was with…No. She was his wife. Ethan wouldn't do anything with her without Harker's permission. The man respected marriage and loyalty above everything except consent.

"Harker calm down and change that contract."

"That isn't going to happen overnight." He needed her home now.

"Then send an email to your lawyer and show her that when she comes home."

"You expect me to sit here and wait while she's out doing whatever in some seedy bar."

"Ellie's with her. Trust me, if they were going anywhere that I was concerned about I'd be with them and not hanging out here with the boys watching the fight."

"Ellie isn't mad at you." He opened his car and got in. He'd go to every club until he found her and then he'd drag her ass home and paddle her for driving him crazy.

"Hey, hold on. Ellie just texted me."

"Tell her to—"

"Shit," said Adrian.

"What's the matter? Are they okay?"

"Yeah, but I have to go."

"Go where? Do you mean you need to get off the phone or are you leaving? Where are you going?"

"You've been hanging out with Alison too long." Adrian laughed.

"Very funny. Where are they?"

"I can't tell you that, but I will tell you that now you should be worried."

"What the fuck does that mean?" He'd already been worried. He pulled his car out of the garage.

"I still can't tell you but think about it." Adrian walked back into the noisy room. "Gotta run fellas. Stay. Have fun. I'll be back later."

"Tell me where they are," he almost shouted.

"You're a smart guy. Where is the one place in the world that you love taking your woman, but you wouldn't want her there without you?"

"I'm in no mood for riddles."

"If I were you, I'd figure it out because at this place she just might decide to suck some guy's dick." Adrian hung up.

"Fuck." Harker tossed his phone on the passenger seat. He hated riddles. He drove down the driveway. He wouldn't want her going to a bad part of town without him, but he wouldn't want to take her there either. He'd take her to a bar or nightclub, but he wouldn't want her going to them without him, especially…His foot slammed on the brakes. "Holy shit. She's at the Club."

Grab your copy of the Baby Battle and find out what happens next.

https://books2read.com/thebabybattle

Thanks for reading **Making the Baby** *(The Billionaire's Baby series book 2).*

Keep reading for an excerpt from book 3, The Baby Battle.

The Baby Battle

"Good evening, ladies." Ethan walked up to them. "I didn't expect to see you here without your partners."

"It's allowed, isn't it?" Ellie smiled at him, but it didn't reach her eyes. "Or am I breaking another rule?"

Alison knew her friend wasn't Ethan's biggest fan, but she had nothing against the man.

"Of course, it's allowed. It's just unexpected." He turned toward Alison. "It's good to see you again." His eyes roamed over her. "You look lovely this evening."

"Thank you." Alison couldn't help it; she blushed. Ethan was so damn hot and what they'd done the last time she'd been here...

"I'm surprised Harker let you out of his sight," he said. "He does have a jealous streak when it comes to you."

"He wasn't happy about it." That was an understatement.

"Does he know you're here?" he asked.

"No, and he doesn't need to," said Ellie. "He doesn't

own her."

"Some laws should've never been changed," muttered Ethan.

Ellie's mouth dropped open.

"Oh, you mean like the one where oral sex was illegal?" Alison tried not to laugh.

"No. Not that law." Ethan frowned but his eyes sparkled with amusement. "That should've never been illegal. Too hard to enforce. I mean, who's going to report it?" He winked at her as his phone buzzed. He pulled it from his pocket and glanced at it. "Excuse me." He turned and walked away.

"That man is such a jerk," said Ellie.

"You're just mad at him because he was pissed that you snuck into the Club. I think he's sweet and sexy as sin."

"Yeah, he's hot but you've never been on the receiving side of his temper. I have. He can be a real ass..." Ellie's eyes widened. "Ah...Alison, as your friend I think you should run."

"What?" She spun around and her stomach dropped to her toes as Harker strode through the crowd toward her.

"I've never seen anyone that angry," whispered Ellie. "I swear I can see steam coming from his ears like in a cartoon."

"Oh...shit." Alison hopped off her seat.

"He won't hurt you, will he?" asked Ellie.

"Ah...no." She didn't think so. "But maybe I should use the restroom." She wasn't proud of it but apparently her fight or flight instinct was flight.

"Good idea." Ellie pushed her. "Go. I'll see if I can stall him."

Alison hurried toward the back hallway.

"Alison, stop," Harker roared.

She froze, glancing over her shoulder as he stormed toward her. "Nope. Not a good idea." She ran through the crowd toward the bathroom.

Grab your copy of the Baby Battle and find out what happens next.

https://books2read.com/thebabybattle

If you sign up for my newsletter, you can get the entire Six Nights of Sin series for free (all six nights of Nick and Sarah's contract—every delicious fantasy) as a thank you gift.

Click here to join and get your free book.

Go to my website or email me for details:

https://www.ellisoday.com/

authorEllisOday@gmail.com

BOOKS BY ELLIS O. DAY
OR SEE THEM ALL ON MY WEBSITE
HTTPS://WWW.ELLISODAY.COM

LA PETITE MORT CLUB SERIES

THE BILLIONAIRE'S BABY
The Billionaire's Baby - The Complete Series:
Books 1-4
https://books2read.com/thebillionairesbaby
The Baby Bargain (book 1) (free)
https://books2read.com/thebabybargain
Making the Baby (book 2)
https://books2read.com/makingthebaby
The Baby Battle (book 3)
https://books2read.com/thebabybattle
Having the Baby (book 4)
https://books2read.com/havingthebaby

HOT HOLIDAYS
Hot Holidays -The Complete Series: Books 1-3
https://books2read.com/hotholidaysseries
The Mistletoe Game (Book 1) (free)
https://mybook.to/mistletoegame
A Banging New Year (Book 2)
https://books2read.com/bangingNewYear

Cupid's Misfire (Book 3)
https://books2read.com/cupidsmisfire

SIX NIGHTS OF SIN SERIES
Six Nights of Sin -The Complete Series: Books 1-6
HTTPS://BOOKS2READ.COM/U/3NEDAR

Interviewing For Her Lover (Book 1) **(Free)**
HTTPS://BOOKS2READ.COM/U/3NYKO6
Taking Control (Book 2)
HTTPS://BOOKS2READ.COM/U/MDKBKR
School Fantasy (Book 3)
HTTPS://BOOKS2READ.COM/U/BP1PER
Master-Slave Fantasy (Book 4)
HTTPS://BOOKS2READ.COM/U/BQZ8JD
Punishment Fantasy (Book 5)
HTTPS://BOOKS2READ.COM/U/MZW9EE
The Proposition (Book 6)
HTTPS://BOOKS2READ.COM/U/3KZR5L

THE VOYEUR SERIES
THE VOYEUR (FREE)
HTTPS://BOOKS2READ.COM/U/BXQBMK
Watching The Voyeur (Book 2)
HTTPS://BOOKS2READ.COM/U/3J0E2J
Touching The Voyeur (Book 3)
HTTPS://BOOKS2READ.COM/U/MGRR66
Loving The Voyeur (Book 4)

HTTPS://BOOKS2READ.COM/U/4AW2PQ

The Voyeur Series (Books 1-4)
HTTPS://BOOKS2READ.COM/U/BZAB9Z

SIX WEEKS OF SEDUCTION
HTTPS://BOOKS2READ.COM/U/3R11YG

A MERRY MASQUERADE FOR CHRISTMAS
HTTPS://BOOKS2READ.COM/U/38R7EV

THE DOM'S SUBMISSION SERIES
The Dom's Submission Box Set (Books 1-3)
HTTPS://BOOKS2READ.COM/U/BA27KQ
His Sub (Book 1) (**Free Ebook**)
HTTPS://BOOKS2READ.COM/U/3YRBLV
His Mission (Book 2)
HTTPS://BOOKS2READ.COM/U/4AQEOO
His Submission (Book 3)
HTTPS://BOOKS2READ.COM/U/49OZED

LA PETITE MORT CLUB INTIMATE ENCOUNTER SERIES
YOU KNOW THE PLAYERS, BUT DO YOU KNOW THE KINK?

HIS LESSON (TERRY AND MAGGIE)
HTTPS://BOOKS2READ.COM/U/4XZPN9

PLAYING HOUSE (NICK AND SARAH)
HTTPS://BOOKS2READ.COM/U/4DYKXK

HIS LOVE (TERRY AND MAGGIE)
HTTPS://BOOKS2READ.COM/U/MGLGZZ

HIS IMPERFECT DAY (TERRY AND MAGGIE)
HTTPS://BOOKS2READ.COM/U/MEEJOV

COMING SOON:

ETHAN'S STORY

MATTIE'S STORY

JAKE'S STORY

REBECCA AND DEREK'S STORY

VIC'S STORY

MITCH'S STORY

RICHARD'S STORY

Email me with questions, concerns or to let me know what you thought of the book. I love hearing from readers.
authorEllisOday@gmail.com

https://www.EllisODay.com

Follow me

Facebook
https://www.facebook.com/EllisODayRomanceAuthor/

Closed FB Group (sneak peeks, sample chapters, and other bonuses)
https://www.facebook.com/groups/153238782143373

Bookbub
https://www.bookbub.com/authors/Ellis-o-day

Instagram
https://www.instagram.com/authorEllisOday/

Twitter
https://twitter.com/Ellis_o_day

Pinterest
www.pinterest.com\AuthorEllisODay

Ellis O. Day

ABOUT THE AUTHOR

Ellis O. Day loves reading and writing about love and sex. She believes that although the two don't have to go together, it's best when they do (both in life and in fantasy).

Ellis O. Day